CY

CHAPARRAL MARAUDERS

D1198458

Presented to

Crosby Branch Library

By

Bruce Ranck
in memory of
Harris County   Wayne Smith
Public Library
your pathway to knowledge

CHAPARRAL MARAUDERS

TOM CURRY

WHEELER
CHIVERS

This Large Print edition is published by Wheeler Publishing, Waterville, Maine, USA and by BBC Audiobooks Ltd, Bath, England.
Wheeler Publishing, a part of Gale, Cengage Learning.
The text of this Large Print edition is unabridged.
Other aspects of the book may vary from the original edition.
Set in 16 pt. Plantin.
Printed on permanent paper.

LIBRARY OF CONGRESS CATALOGING-IN-PUBLICATION DATA

Curry, Tom, 1900–
    Chaparral mauraders / by Tom Curry. — Large print ed.
    p. cm. — (Wheeler Publishing large print western)
    Originally published: New York : Modern Literary Editions, 1939.
    ISBN-13: 978-1-59722-971-5 (softcover : alk. paper)
    ISBN-10: 1-59722-971-7 (softcover : alk. paper)
    1. Texas—Fiction. 2. Large type books. I. Title.
    PS3505.U9725C47 2009
    813'.52—dc22   2009002066

BRITISH LIBRARY CATALOGUING-IN-PUBLICATION DATA AVAILABLE

Published in 2009 in the U.S. by arrangement with Golden West Literary Agency.
Published in 2009 in the U.K. by arrangement with Golden West Literary Agency.

U.K. Hardcover: 978 1 408 44184 8 (Chivers Large Print)
U.K. Softcover: 978 1 408 44185 5 (Camden Large Print)

Printed in the United States of America
1 2 3 4 5 6 7 13 12 11 10 09

Chaparral Marauders

CHAPTER I
LAW OF THE BUSH

Vast and thorny, the jungles of the Nueces spread for miles in every direction, hemming in the party of murderous men who rode the twisting trails southwest from Mescal town, capital of newly formed Chaparral County, Texas.

This jungle was a strange world, a universe in itself, a Gargantuan brier patch where the thorns were inches long, sharp enough to impale a man. A couple of dozen tough, hard-faced riders slowly pushed through the winding way. In the lead was the big, fierce-eyed Sheriff Grole whose long and bony legs, cased in leather to ward off the myriad thorns, gripped the barrel ribs of his handsome chestnut stallion.

"Make it quiet, boys," the sheriff growled — he had a voice that grated roughly. "Somebuddy's up ahead there. Mebbe another outlaw to add to our collection."

The bush swarmed with fugitives who ran

to its shelter from the law, men of the Owl-hoot Trail to whom the impenetrable thickets and mazes afforded a welcome haven. Other wild creatures abounded in the chaparral; long-horned, lean-flanked steers as fast and feral as any cougar, who fed in the night and lay quiet during the day; wild boars with great tusks, ready to fight at the sight of man. Nice country.

"We oughta make Gregory's ranch by noon, Sheriff," one of the officer's aides remarked. "And ain't yuh intendin' to hit Thorny Woods soon, too?"

"Plenty of time for them," replied the sheriff gruffly. "We kin use more men."

Sheriff Pat Grole had not shaved for several days, and the beard stubble was wiry and black on the jutting chin and high-boned cheeks. There were red glints in his eyes which were set a bit too close together for pleasantness over the high, sharp bridge of the eagle beak. He was burnt by the Texas sun till his skin was dark as a Mexican's.

Clad in gray shirt and pants, on his vest was pinned his badge of authority as sheriff of Chaparral. In the brush he wore, as did his followers, heavy smooth leather chaps and leather gloves, while his stirrups were fronted by *tapaderos* to protect the feet and shins from black thorns.

The aromatic scent of mesquite and other blooms hung in the dry air. Off to the west a sudden, sharp "pop" sounded, not unlike a cork being drawn from an effervescing bottle; a wild cow, a "brush-popper," disturbed by man's approach, was hitting the wall of chaparral to escape.

"Hear that?" said Grole curtly. "That there cow ran outa the way of the rider ahead. He'll be close, boys, and his hoss is lame."

The ugly black eyes sought the trail again. Fresh hoofprints, one showing the steel shoe on a fore hoof to be split, led Grole on. He was a good tracker and could read sign, knew the man before them was not too expert a horseman since he had allowed the stone to work in and split that shoe at some past time, causing the beast to go lame. This was the sort of error for which a man on the dodge would pay with his life, the kind of mistake a greenhorn would make.

"Take that branch, Dinny," ordered Grole, "and yuh kin cut him off if he hears us. Ride, now."

He dug in his own spurs, pulling a black-steeled six-shooter, the wooden stock of which was corrugated with notches, each nick meaning a foe buried with boots on. The pistol was a Frontier Model Colt .45, and Grole handled it with the practiced ease of an expert. The chestnut stallion, nostrils flaring wide so the light in the thin membrane made them seem red as blood, eyes rolling to the whites, ears flat as he felt the tearing rollers of the spurs in his flanks, galloped in and out along the winding trail; he was a trained brush horse that knew how to run that jungle chaparral.

Whirling around a corner, Grole saw in a small natural clearing a pale-faced, alarmed young man who had been attempting to fasten his saddle cinch. Grole shouted hoarsely, fired a slug that made a hole in the youth's Stetson and sent his hands quickly up above his curly, light-haired head. The sheriff reined his chestnut to a halt, the crows-feet at the corners of his ugly eyes deepening as he looked the lad over.

"Unbuckle and drap," he ordered, six-gun trained on the stranger's breast bone. "I'm sheriff of this county and I kin see what *yore* callin' is."

The misery in the youth's eyes was pitiful; anybody but a person of Grole's coarse caliber would have been touched by it.

"Aw right, Sheriff," replied the prisoner, voice low. "Guess yuh got me. But my gun's empty —"

"Unbuckle," repeated Grole. "I wanta talk

to yuh."

Thin as a rail, obviously starved and weak from a long flight, the prisoner passed a shaky hand across his eyes and reeled back as he unfastened the belt of his Colt. The holstered weapon fell with a soft swish to the grass while Grole's extraordinary tough looking possemen formed an armed circle about the prisoner.

"Where yuh from?" demanded Grole. "And what's yore handle."

The youth hesitated, then, as Grole threateningly shifted his gun, he answered:

"Oklahoma, town of Durant. My name's Tim Haggerty."

"What they want yuh up there for?"

The unhappy eyes fell; in a low voice he said, "Murder."

"How much reward?"

"Five hundred dollars," he whispered, then added, "But Sheriff, I never done that shootin', honest. It's a mistake. I —"

Grole chuckled sneeringly, and the laugh went around the ring. "That's what they all say," the sheriff commented. "Now listen, keerful: s'pose I told yuh that 'stead of shippin' yore hide back to Oklahoma I mean to give yuh a ridin' job with me. Stick along and yuh'll never be arrested in this county, savvy. Onct we're through here, I'll let yuh

11

go yore way, and if yuh've done well I'll even pay yuh for workin'. The boys with me 'll tell yuh I'm talkin' truth, eh, boys?"

There was a chorus of assent from Grole's men. Hope flashed into the boy's eyes as he raised them to the sheriff's brutal face. "Yuh really mean that, Mister? Yuh'll make a deppity outa me? Shore, I'll be glad tuh work for yuh."

"And do what I say? It's man's work, outlaw. Yuh kin handle a gun and yuh shouldn't mind killin', as yuh're wanted for murder."

"I'll do anything that's right," agreed Tim Haggerty stoutly. "Really I'm not a bandit and killer. I was framed up there in Durant. I jist wanta be honest and decent, so —"

"Aw, he means it; he's no good to us, Sheriff," snarled a heavy-jowled gunman. "He'd never shoot anybuddy — our way."

Haggerty stared in horror at the round black eye of death. Grole swung on him.

"No, don't shoot me, Sheriff — my mother'll never git over it —"

The staccato roar of the Colt in Grole's paw cut him off short as the sound bellowed through the wilderness. A blue hole appeared squarely between the tragic, dark eyes. And young Haggerty silently folded up, dead at the dancing hoofs of the chestnut stallion.

"Easier to tote dead," remarked Grole, letting his gun slide back into its oiled holster. "Shove him back in the bush and pile some rocks over him to keep the caracaras and coyotes from pickin' at him. We'll tote him to town on our way back and git the five hunderd."

"Shore glad I didn't feel the way he did 'bout jinin' yore crew, Sheriff," remarked a fat hombre dryly, and the others laughed.

"He'd never've backed yuh against these fool ranchers," said another. "Let's get on. I'm honin' for the gun-fightin' to begin, Grole."

"Yuh'll have yore wish," the sheriff growled, "and pronto. I guess I got plenty of gunmen outa this bush to do the job. We're ready for the final clean-up."

A mile to the northwest, skirting the Ruby Hills which rose in the western part of Chaparral County, from a high point two riders looked down across the distant country.

The man in advance, mounted on a magnificent black stallion, wore a black sombrero straight on his dark-haired, handsome head. Though his weight was around 200 pounds, so beautifully proportioned was the tall rider that he seemed not at all large until compared to other men. Broad shoulders, covered by a flowing black cape which as it flew back in the wind of speed showed the two heavy, well-kept .45 revolvers, tapered to the narrow waist of a fighting man.

The upper part of his face was concealed by a black domino mask, the blue eyes gleaming steadily through the slits, while the exposed jaw was firm, set with determination. This man, both cursed and praised all over the West, was the individual known as the Masked Rider.

"Did yuh hear that shot, Blue Hawk?" he called back to his copper-skinned companion, who rode with the accomplished native ease of the Indian on the gray horse.

"Si, Senor," nodded the Yaqui. "I hear. Think mebbe trouble."

"Yeah, yuh're right. There's a bunch of riders down below. We better hurry, or we'll never get that kid back to his mother."

The Masked Rider spoke at the black stallion's sensitive ear; and Midnight paced swiftly on through the winding bush trail.

A Legend of the rangeland, the name of the Masked Rider was anathema to hard-faced hombres. Outlaws hated his guts for they feared the flaming guns of the Robin Hood outlaw who fought only for the

14

decent people. They shrank before the indomitable, grim fighter who battled for the oppressed though he was an outlaw with a high price on his own rugged, handsome head.

No one knew this man's real identity, not even the Yaqui Indian, Blue Hawk, his constant companion and helper who followed the Masked Rider into the face of death, without any hesitancy, without questioning. Blue Hawk was tall, with the Indian's high cheekbones; his lithe body was loosely cased in cotton drill pants and shirt, white save for a bright red sash and headband holding his long straight black hair. In the sash Blue Hawk had his long knife stuck; a Winchester rifle rode his saddle boot. Blue Hawk, faithful to the end, knew the Masked Rider only as Wayne Morgan, the wandering waddy disguise which the great bandit assumed when he wished to approach people during one of his investigations.

"I'd hate," remarked the Masked Rider, "to miss that kid now, Blue Hawk, after the long trail we've made from Oklahoma. Promised his family I'd see he got back safe. We worked mighty hard to prove he was really innocent of that murder charge."

Blue Hawk said nothing; he understood.

He knew how this strange outlaw, who was a legend from the Rio Grande to the Columbia River, felt about the Owl-hoot Trail. Fate had dealt cruelly with the Masked Rider; crimes he had never committed were blamed on him, bank robberies, hold-ups and murders, awful atrocities, so he had lost hope of ever vindicating himself.

It was from this very life into which he himself had been forced that the Masked Rider sought to save young Tim Haggerty. A man had been killed in Durant, Oklahoma, during a robbery; evidence had been planted by an enemy of Haggerty's and the youth had fled from arrest. Wayne Morgan had caught the real culprit and set out on the lad's trail, following that split horseshoe that had gradually grown worse until Haggerty's horse was lamed.

"I've got to save him from livin' the way I do," muttered the Masked Rider.

He expected no reward for what he did in helping the downtrodden; only his soul found gratification in fighting for the under-dog, and that along his back trail might be found many who would ever hold the name of the Masked Rider in veneration. This made his life worthwhile, as he rode his mysterious way, his real story unfathomed.

Eternally vigilant, the Masked Rider

shoved through the thorny chaparral in the direction of that gunshot. He raised a hand and Blue Hawk slowed the gray and put a brown hand on the rifle under his leg. Carefully the pair of them entered the little clearing where, only a half hour ago, death had struck.

Now the clearing was empty. Grole and his "posse" had ridden on. But young Tim Haggerty's trail ended here.

"Keep guard, Blue Hawk," the Masked Rider ordered.

He dismounted, casting about for sign. He found the crushed grass where the youth had fallen, the blackish blood spots where his head had lain, the track where the body had been dragged to the cairn. . . .

"Shot down in cold blood," he muttered, as he finished his swift, efficient survey. The gun belt was off; the Haggerty pistol was not even loaded. "That boy would never have shot anybody, anyway," he went on, staring for a moment into the sad, coal-black eyes of the Yaqui.

CHAPTER II
AT THE GREGORY
RANCH

For a few moments more the Masked Rider cast about, lips grimly keen, identifying the hoofmarks of the various riders who had done this.

"A couple of dozen of 'em," he growled. "C'mon, we'll trail 'em."

The black-clad hombre sprang into Midnight's saddle and pushed on, trailed by the wary Yaqui. He rode with the ease of an accomplished bronc-buster and puncher, and the way Midnight handled himself in the chaparral showed he had traveled such country before.

To the southwest, a flock of black specks rose, winging off to one side against the hot blue sky. Crows, flying from the party in advance. It marked the positon of the killers.

Cold fury was in the Masked Rider's heart, fury against the men who had made it impossible for him to keep his promise to

Tim Haggerty's mother about fetching back the young fellow. He knew there had been no legitimate excuse for the shooting of Haggerty.

Grole had taken the lame horse, with the telltale split shoe, along with him. The trail was simple, and the Masked Rider grimly followed it with Blue Hawk.

"Rancho," grunted the Yaqui at length.

"Yeah, yuh're right, Blue Hawk. Let's git in closer; better take that branch trail and come in from the other way."

They had circled to the south on side trails, and finally approached the clearing in which the bush ranch stood. Sitting their horses in the chaparral, they looked through a gap and took in the sun-blackened barn, the 'dobe and brush shacks, the white-brick barn ranchhouse in its yard.

A sunbeam glinted on the silver badge pinned to Sheriff Grole's vest. The county officer had dismounted, and his men with him, two holding the reins of the horses in hand while the remaining businesslike gunmen grouped alongside their master Grole.

They were facing a party of brush-poppers, isolated ranchers of the chaparral country. The Masked Rider observed the stocky, white-haired father, with three stalwart waddies at his back. In the house doorway stood the rancher's wife and a couple of young women, evidently daughters of the elderly couple.

"Yuh're through down here, Gregory; yuh got to light out," boomed the sheriff's harsh voice. "Yore title ain't wuth two bits since yuh failed to register in the new county."

"Yuh're crazy," cried the oldster. "I done filed in Webb County twenty-five years back!"

"Yeah, but the law says if yuh didn't re-file in Chaparral inside thutty days, others kin claim yore land. That's bin done, it belongs to someone else who's demandin' his property. Pack and ride. I'm on'y carryin' out my orders, 'cordin' to law."

"If it's like that," snarled the brush-popper, "I say damn the law —"

The fight broke in a flash, begun by one of Grole's vicious deputies who shoved the old rancher roughly. A waddy jumped in to protect his boss, one of the cowboy's hands coming near his gun. Grole's pistol spurted red death, bullet driving through the waddy's belly and folding him up, a writhing horror who squealed with anguish as he died.

Gregory uttered a curse of righteous indignation at the scarcely veiled murder of his man; a woman screamed shrilly, and bravely the old rancher grabbed for his shooting iron, his two remaining men acting with him. Surrounded by killers, they would be wiped out. The sheriff, a wizard on the draw, swift as a rattler's striking head, swung his black gun muzzle to kill Gregory.

"Cover from the bush, Blue Hawk," snapped the Masked Rider, as he started away.

Midnight bounded into the clearing, charging Grole's gang from the rear. A slug, whipping from the big six-shooter of the Masked Rider as he attacked, caught the killer of the waddy between the shoulder blades, and the gunny's arms flew out, pistol leaving his relaxed fingers as he arched back, face screwed up in the agony of death.

The sharp report of the black-clad outlaw's Colt startled Grole and his men. The sheriff's second shot, designed for old Gregory's heart, was deflected by the slight jerk of the officer's arm at the boom of Morgan's Colt. Gregory took it through the upper arm, the shock knocking him to his knees, blood spurting to his shirt. A member of the posse received a bullet through the brain as the gunnies swung to face the unexpected threat from their rear.

"The Masked Rider!" shrieked Grole. "Git him, boys — there's a ten-thousand-dollar reward for him."

The killers jumped toward the oncoming outlaw. The Masked Rider's intervention gave Gregory's remaining men the seconds they needed in which to pick up their wounded boss, hurry over to the house. They left the dead man in the yard.

With flaming guns the Masked Rider drove at the array of Grole's deadly bunch. From the thorny bush behind the black stallion a rifle cracked, and a slug intended for the outlaw merely clipped through the crown of his black hat, as Blue Hawk shot down a cool-headed gunman who was kneeling for better aim.

Realizing that in the bright daylight the massed "deputies" could kill him, the Masked Rider, having accomplished his purpose of saving the Gregorys for the moment, swerved the black stallion. Bullets tore the air in his wake, nipping the black clothing, shrieking hate in his ears. The wall of dry chaparral stood solid before him, but Midnight never hesitated. The giant stallion threw himself sideward and hit the brush, a loud "pop" cracking out as he smashed through.

Long thorns tore at leather, at the hide of the animal. Down low, along the magnificent, arched neck, the Masked Rider urged his pet on. The pursuing bullets zipped into the bush blindly; the law could no longer see him.

"Git goin' after him — grab yore hosses!" bellowed Grole.

By main strength Midnight tore a path through the black chaparral. Every kind of cruelly thorned bush grew here in a luxuriant, tangled mass; catclaw and granjeno, greasewood and dagger, the dense mesquite with its white blooms, prickly-pear with its green-and-yellow fruit, and coarse chino grass filled the lower spaces.

Many plants were in flower; the creosote with yellow blossoms and pungent odor reeking in the warm air, the ratama, and in the flats cacti, wandlike ocotillos, yucca, cholla with needle-sharp, deformed arms. Ridges of the land were covered with the mescal stalks, thirty feet high, here and there a feathery huisache tree fought with the rest of the vegetation for light and water, the breeze waving the sea of chaparral like the land ocean it was.

Diverted from the massacre they had planned for the Gregory men, Grole and his posse, mouths watering for the big rewards many counties had posted for the Masked Rider, dead or alive, leaped on their horses and took after him.

The black-clad hombre looked back over his shoulder, as thorned branches reached for him, threatening to drag him from his seat.

"Reckon I'll draw 'em away," he muttered, "and give those pore folks a chance!"

The Masked Rider was worth a small fortune to Sheriff Pat Grole. And after killing a couple of Grole's men, the Masked Rider could never hope for anything less than a fight to the death.

Midnight's driving hoofs sunk deep into the swampy, darker earth surrounding a *resaca*, a marshy lake hidden in the chaparral jungle. Flocks of birds rose with raucous cries from around the water as the giant black stallion, guided by the soothing voice of his rider, skirted the edges of the pond, formed by the little stream which was the source of the nearby ranch's water supply.

Listening intently, as the birds winged away and it grew quieter, the Masked Rider could hear the heavy crashings and curses of Grole and his gunmen as they laboriously followed his trail through the brush. Forced westward by the *resaca*, the black-clad hombre, strong chin set, led Grole farther and farther off.

He had overheard Grole's declaration of the new law which deprived the rancher of his claim and home; it sounded like a sharp legal trick.

"Wonder how far they're goin' — and why," he muttered. Anger at the big sheriff burned in his heart, at the cold-blooded murder of young Haggerty, at Grole's obvious brutality in enforcing the so-called law.

"Them fellers look more like bandits than possemen," he decided.

Now and then as they topped a mesquite ridge, the pursuers glimpsed the outlaw ahead; they would whoop and shoot, at long range, toward the Masked Rider. Coolly he paid no attention as the slugs bit the brush around him; only a lucky one might strike its mark.

For an hour he led them on, ever westward. The sun kissed the red-topped hills slightly north, so that they shone with the splendor of gigantic rubies.

Midnight at last hit a narrow, winding trail and began making swifter time along it. Grole and his bunch dropped farther and farther behind, finally stopped, allowing the Masked Rider to pause for a rest. The giant stallion's lathered ribs heaved. Thorns had torn his legs and sides, and trickles of blood were running down the velvet black coat.

The Masked Rider, eyes gleaming behind the domino mask, stared back toward the spot where the sheriff retreated. As quiet descended over the chaparral, in the west distance he heard dim sounds, the calls of men. He dismounted and watered Midnight at the little brook which emptied the *resaca* he had passed. Then he found a small clearing, hidden from the trail, and squatted there to wait patiently.

It was dark when he heard the eerie cry of a mountain lion — the signal by which the Yaqui and he always got together after being unexpectedly separated. He answered, the mournful sound ringing in the black chaparral. All about him were mysterious stirrings, the night life of the bush. Wild steers were cautiously moving down to water and feed, and the raiders of the darkness were on the prowl.

Blue Hawk, on his gray horse, slid up the trail, and silently dismounted at the Masked Rider's side. The white suit of his Indian friend outlined Blue Hawk against the brush as the Masked Rider spoke in low tones.

"Yuh watched those ranchers, Blue Hawk? What happened?"

"All go, quick," Blue Hawk replied. "Escape, Senor."

"I don't like that sheriff's way," growled the Masked Rider. "If what he says is true 'bout that land law, the folks in these parts need help. Wonder how big a gang Grole's got?"

"Senor, I see more come from north. Beeg bunch. All bad men, no good."

The Masked Rider made his decision. "There's a ranch not far above here. I'll take yore horse and go up there as Wayne Morgan and find out what goes on in these parts."

Blue Hawk nodded; he squatted silently on the ground as the Masked Rider quickly took off his mask and black clothing, rolled the articles into a tight bundle and bound it behind the saddle inside an ordinary cowpuncher's poncho. He put on his other outfit, revealing a head of thick dark hair as he removed the black Stetson, replacing it with a battered gray hat. Dark-colored Levi's thrust into worn cowboy boots, blue shirt with bright bandanna knotted loosely at his throat completed the change in costume which altered the Robin Hood outlaw's looks radically. He now appeared to be a wandering waddy, toting the usual complement of heavy Colt .45s tied low on his hips in their supple holsters.

"Stay close enough so yuh kin hear my call," he ordered Blue Hawk. "Rest Midnight. I'll take care of the gray."

"Si, Senor," agreed the Yaqui solemnly.

CHAPTER III
THE RABBIT LEG
OUTFIT

An hour later Wayne Morgan saw through the brush the lights of a big ranch. It was the one from which had come the sounds he had heard that afternoon. A red fire licked hungrily into the night sky, lighting up the big clearing, and outlining the rambling adobe house with its long, shaded porch, and the stables and barns, corrals and bunk house.

Approaching a closed gate, Wayne Morgan saw stalking sentinels, ready rifles gripped in hand. The nearest, a man in cowboy clothing, had heard the noise of his open approach, and the Winchester clicked as the barrel rose to cover the incoming rider.

"Who's that?" called the waddy.

"A friend," Wayne Morgan replied.

"Come on, but come slow and with yore hands where I kin see 'em."

The ranch was on guard, alert. Over the

gate, which was opened as he came up to it, Morgan saw a rough signboard, with white lettering and the painted symbol of a rabbit.

"RABBIT LEG RANCH," the printed words proclaimed.

Armed cowboys instantly bunched around the newcomer, staring suspiciously, curiously.

"Who are yuh?" demanded the man with the Winchester.

"Name's Morgan — Wayne Morgan. Just a wanderin' waddy, pard. Am I too late for grubpile?"

"Go on up to the house," ordered the guard curtly.

Eyes fixed him, silently. He dismounted, calmly, sizing them up. A great, hearty voice, which had the timbre of a bull's roar, sang out from the shadows of the house veranda.

"Who the hell's that, Shorty?"

Down the steps came an old brush-popper rancher. He approached with the stiff gait and swagger of a man born to leather. In the firelight Morgan read him instantly as a chief and leader of men. At first glance, with his pepper-and-salt beard and white hair covered by a brown Stetson, figure straight and strong, with powerful chest and thick waist, he did not seem very old. He was chewing tobacco, the alligator hide of his seamed cheek working in unison with his jaw motion.

"Feller says he's jist a wanderin' cowpoke, Boss," said Shorty, the hombre covering Morgan. There was a slight touch of sarcasm that set the tall newcomer on guard.

The boss looked him over, seemed satisfied, though his cracked lips twitched a bit with that same amusement Shorty showed. "All right, Mr. Wanderer. Yuh kin quit wanderin' and squat. Yuh're welcome at the Rabbit Leg. Yuh know me?"

"No sir," Morgan replied truthfully.

"My name's Jim Woods — folks call me Thorny."

Jim "Thorny" Woods was close to seventy years, but he was apparently as salty and hard as he had ever been. The big, long nose, the jut of his bearded jaw, the fire in his washed-out blue eyes which were the color of a pale summer sky, told Wayne Morgan that the old rancher was stubborn, honest, and a real fighter.

Thorny Woods didn't ask any more questions. That was against the code of the brush-poppers, and another reason why the chaparral was in such favor as a hiding-place for men on the dodge. All ranchers would feed strangers and never tell the law.

"We got a house full tonight — some neighbors come in," drawled Thorny Woods. "But plenty of room in the barn, stranger. There's grub in the kitchen. So long as yuh behave yoreself, yuh kin stay long as yuh like."

He nodded briefly, turned on his heel, and went back into the house. The front door opened, and Morgan glimpsed a small, dainty-figured young woman. Her beauty held him, fascinated him. He almost caught his breath at the loveliness of her face under the dark, curly hair, the clear light of her eyes.

"Grandfather," she said, "I wish you'd come in and rest yourself."

"Aw right, Louise," the old brush-popper replied, mildly.

In the house Morgan could see Gregory, with his arm in a rough bandage. He had saved the old rancher from death, and evidently, taking advantage of the lull afforded by the Masked Rider, the womenfolk and survivors had hurried to the neighboring Rabbit Leg Ranch for succor in their distress.

"You folks seem on the prod," Morgan said to Shorty. "Kin I help?"

The cowboy shrugged, the offer of aid seeming to please him. From what he next

31

said, Morgan guessed what they believed him, a rather bedraggled stranger on a thorn-scratched gray horse, to be.

"The sheriff down here, his name's Pat Grole, is makin' us turrible trouble — but don't worry, we won't turn yuh in to him." Obviously, they thought him a law-dodger so common in the bush.

"I'm not partial to sheriffs, 'specially men like Grole," Morgan admitted.

"Didn't figger yuh would be. This one's a sidewinder if ever there was one. He's throwin' folks off their ranches wholesale, and he's killed a dozen or more that we know of. He claims it's on 'count of a crooked law we never heard tell of. But they can't skeer our boss. Folks're lookin' to him for help."

"Why would they wanta grab this range?" asked Morgan.

Shorty shrugged, as he led the stranger to the grub shack. "Dunno. We never was bothered afore. Grole's got a bunch of killers outa the bush, sworn 'em in as possemen to do the dirty work here."

The gray was cared for. Morgan ate, and turned in to sleep in the fragrant hay of a mow in the barn loft. For a time he lay awake, staring through the cracks between sun-dried, shrunken boards at the glow of the fire.

He thought of pretty Louise Woods, and his mouth became grim. Not for him could there ever be a home with such a prize as a good woman at his side; he was condemned forever to be a wanderer, hunted by greedy-eyed hombres for the blood money on his head.

He shut these bitter thoughts from his mind, and went to sleep.

The sun was rising when the Masked Rider awoke. But it was not the light which had roused him. Instead it was the heavy tread of many horses approaching the Rabbit Leg Ranch. Right below him he heard low voices, and the familiar click of cocking guns. He silently pulled himself from the soft, sweet hay, walked along a twelve-inch beam over to the half-open mow door commanding the scene below.

It seemed deserted, peaceful. But coming into the yard was a band of fifty men, led by Sheriff Pat Grole. They were heavily armed. Grole, his ugly face staring at the seemingly sleeping house, paused at the gate.

"Hey — Jim Woods!" sang out the sheriff.

The house door opened, and Thorny Woods stepped out on the porch.

"What yuh want, Grole?" he roared.

"Come out here. I wanta talk to yuh."

"Yuh kin come into the yard — but come alone, if yuh wanta talk."

With a muttered curse, Grole swung down from his saddle and opened the gate. He gave a low order to his tough looking men from the side of his mouth. Halfway to the house he paused, facing Woods, who came down to meet him, stopping half a dozen paces from the tall sheriff.

"I wanta see yore warranty to this land," stated Sheriff Grole heavily.

Thorny Woods' old lips twitched; he patted the six-shooter at his hip.

"There's my warranty, Grole," he answered. "Ain't she a beauty?"

"Now look here," growled the sheriff. "Quit foolin', Woods. The law says yuh got to register yore claims. There's bin a deed filed in Chaparral County claimin' this here stretch."

Thorny Woods laughed. "I never did file, even in Webb, Sheriff. This land is mine. I lived here sixty years. Figger I don't need any help to keep it."

"Yuh're a loco old fool," snapped Grole. "I'll give yuh jist one hour to pack up and git, Woods. It's the law speakin'. I'm on'y enforcin' it, as I'm paid to do."

34

"Reckon yuh're bein' paid all right," Thorny Woods drawled, "but by whom? As for one hour, I don't need it to say I ain't movin'."

Grole made a quick gesture with his right arm; the crowd of armed deputies surged through the gate.

"Yuh're outa luck, Woods," the sheriff cried. "This land's somebuddy else's now. I arrest yuh for obstructin' justice —"

Wayne Morgan's hand rested on the butt of his six-shooter. From the move Grole made, stepping back, he figured the sheriff meant to draw. Thorny Woods figured so, too, and his hand shot out, seized Grole by the wrist, his bearded jaw sticking into his enemy's face.

An excited gunman let off his rifle, and the bullet whirled over the two men in the center of the yard, plugging into the house wall. Right below, in the barn, Morgan heard the bark of another gun, and the posseman who had fired, yipped and let go his Winchester to claw at his punctured shoulder. Wily Thorny Woods had a bunch of waddies hidden inside the barn.

Grole cursed, stopped his play, glaring into the seamed blue eyes of Thorny Woods, who was laughing in his face.

"Yuh gotta git up earlier than this to

s'prise us," said Woods. He indicated the barn, where bristling gun muzzles covered the halted gang of gunmen behind Grole. "More warranties, Sheriff."

Then the old man's voice grew grim, steely. "Now keep away from here, savvy? Yuh've bin ridin' high, wide and handsome in the chaparral, but yuh're goin' to quit and leave us folks be. We're peaceable but we'll fight to the end for our rights. Gregory's here and a bunch of other friends of mine're bandin' together, people yuh've beat and shot up and run off'n their ranches. Next time you won't git off so easy."

Grole was livid, foaming with rage, his yellowed teeth gritted.

"Aw right — I'm goin', Woods. But I'll be back. Yuh've failed to register yore title within the thutty days as required by the law of Chaparral County. The hull might of the law is behind me."

"I'm for the law," snapped Thorny Woods. "But when a skunk like you tries to use it to ruin pore and decent folks, that's diff'rent. Now git, and take yore bandits with yuh."

He swung the powerful, heavy sheriff, gave him a shove.

"I'll see yuh die for that," snarled Grole.

"Go on — start," roared Thorny Woods. "Let's see me die now."

But Grole didn't like the menacing guns trained on him; he hesitated to give the attack order. Instead, he stalked quickly to the gate, mounted, and waved his pack of gunnies off. Catcalls from the triumphant waddies followed the passel of riders as they dwindled out of sight in the chaparral.

Hired hands and ranchers of the county, came out of hiding to join Woods. The old brush-popper's face was grave as Wayne Morgan, sliding down the ladder, went outside to the group in the middle of the yard.

"Grole'll be back, boys. We'll hafta be ready to fight 'em," Woods declared.

Just what the whole mess was all about, Morgan had yet to learn, but it was obvious that ruin and death stared these independent ranchers in the face. Undoubtedly there were powerful forces at work behind Sheriff Grole, or he never would have dared to organize outlaws as his possemen and boldly attempt to dispossess from their homes these men who had won their ranches by hard labor and sweat.

Morgan proceeded to stroll around and mingle with the folks gathered at the Rabbit Leg ranch, endeavoring to pick up bits of information for his future guidance. He found that during the night half a dozen more groups of shattered ranchers had ridden in to the Rabbit Leg Ranch, to ask for protection and help from Jim Thorny Woods. They had brought their womenfolk and children along, and there was not one family that had not lost a son or relative by legalized gunman's bullet. They told harrowing tales of brutality; even those who had left their homes immediately when ordered to do so, had been beaten up by the cold-blooded "deputies." These refugees, sadness and shock written on their faces, overflowed the big house and the barns, and tents made of wagon sheets were improvised in the yard.

Food was needed. Wayne Morgan's heart warmed to the old rancher when he heard Thorny Woods order a couple of men to go drive in a half-dozen beeves for butchering to feed the dispossessed people.

Morgan concluded, from the stories he heard, that at least two hundred deputies were in the neighborhood; Grole had split them into bands, sending them here and there to take over the ranches. But the bush seemed quiet, somnolent, with no menace in it, as Woods' two brush-poppers saddled up and rode out to pick up some steers for meat.

An hour passed. Then Morgan heard a

single wail, a low animal call, the perfectly simulated mountain lion signal of Blue Hawk. He strolled to the edge of the yard, leaned on the fence rail. The wall of bush looked quite blank, but when he had been there for a few minutes, he heard the Yaqui's whisper:

"Senor, the sheriff has kill the two who ride from here!"

"Where's Grole now?" Morgan asked, without moving.

Blue Hawk, in careful voice that reached only the ears of his tall friend, informed Morgan that Grole was to the south of the Rabbit Leg, and that more and more parties of heavily armed men were joining him. There were, stated Blue Hawk, already over a hundred fighters with Grole. They had caught the two Rabbit Leg waddies and throttled them as the cowboys dismounted to secure a steer they had roped.

"Keep an eye on them, Blue Hawk, and let me know when they move," Morgan ordered. "Reckon Grole's usin' killer bandits here, sayin' they're depitties. They've come in mighty thick."

Though the yard was crowded with cowboys and ranchers, no one had overheard the whispered colloquy. Morgan swung, face stern, toward the house, in time to see two men who had been let through the guards at the north trail. He eased over, as the people stared at the newcomers.

CHAPTER IV
BLOODY BRUSH

Both new arrivals were obviously dudes, easterners. One was a stalwart young man in khaki, brown shirt open at the neck, army pants tucked into high-laced brown boots, an army Stetson, set straight on his light, curly hair. His brown eyes were wide-set and very frank, over a straight nose and pleasant mouth; he made a handsome picture of youth as he stood there, gratefully accepting the cool dipper of well-water Louise Woods handed him. He smiled at the pretty young woman and Morgan saw the roses glow in her cheeks.

Thorny Woods boomed, "Yuh'll find the Ruby Hills jist two miles west of here, young feller."

"Thanks, sir. My name's Robert Harrison, and this is David Rose. I come from Chicago. We lost our way above here, and saw your smoke. If it's all right, we'll rest a little while before riding on."

"Shore it's aw right," Woods said heartily. "There's food if yuh want it. Make yourself at home."

Rose, the other pilgrim, was older, a middle-aged, colorless man with sandy hair and a sallow face. Gray frosted his temples, and his movements seemed nervous, ill at ease. He wore the same kind of clothing as Harrison, and strapped behind his saddle was a black leather kit.

"Won't you come in?" asked Louise. "There's some hot coffee on the stove."

The two entered the ranchhouse, and Morgan eased up to Thorny Woods.

"I heard a couple shots a few minutes ago, Woods," he said, keeping his voice low so as not to alarm the womenfolk. "Reckon Grole isn't so far off. Yuh s'pose he's grabbed yore two waddies yuh sent for beef?"

The old brush-popper scowled, forehead corrugated with wrinkles. "Mebbe so. I thought that sidewinder'd left for the time bein'."

"Next time yuh want beef, better send plenty of men for guards," counseled Morgan.

"Yuh're right. Now who the hell's this comin'?"

The seamed blue eyes of the rancher turned to the north gate. "Why, the bush is lousy with dudes today," he growled. "Here come two more!"

On lathered horses the latest newcomers were let through the guards. They were dressed like Harrison and Rose. One was tall and slender, with dark-brown hair, and a quick, darting way of using his slate-colored eyes. He had a sharp nose and smoothly shaved, high-boned cheeks, an intelligent look to him. His companion was very large, a raw-boned Scandinavian, with tow hair and a pink, round face.

Thorny Woods greeted them with his usual hearty hospitality.

"My name's Albert LaSalle," the slender man said. "I'm from Tucson, sir, representing the Arizona Syndicate."

The Swede with him was Oley King, a man of few words, taciturn, unperturbed by the stares of the curious cattlemen.

Morgan could read the card which La-Salle handed Thorny Woods, who turned the little white pasteboard in his calloused fingers. *"Albert LaSalle: Arizona Mining Syndicate. Tucson."*

"Mining?" exclaimed Thorny Woods. "Yuh're purty hopeful if yuh're huntin' mines in these parts, Mister. I've lived here man and boy for sixty years and never heard tell of any mines wuth botherin' with."

43

LaSalle smiled, shrugged. "I'm on my way to the Ruby Hills," he said. "They're near here, aren't they?"

"They are — right over there. Yuh kin see the tops from the porch." Thorny Woods waved to the red-crested mountains westward. "They shore seem pop'lar jist now. Two more dudes're hunting 'em. They're inside the house now."

"What!" cried LaSalle, startled. "Who are they?"

"Yuh kin see 'em for yoreself. One says his name's Harrison, the other's Rose."

LaSalle shot his companion a worried look. "That's Bob Harrison of the Chicago Mining Corporation, King! And David Rose is the best assayer in the country! We've got to make the hills before they do. C'mon."

The slender man hustled from the porch and mounted his lathered horse. Followed by Oley King, he spurred toward the trail which led to the hills.

Bob Harrison came out, quickly. "What was that?" he demanded.

"Feller named LaSalle — here's his kyard," growled Thorny Woods. "He ain't as perlite as he might be; never even said adios."

Harrison glanced quickly at the card. He clicked his lips and showed the same perturbation LaSalle had evinced when he heard about Harrison's presence.

"Rose," he called. "Come, hurry up, or we'll be beaten to it." He swung, young face serious, to thank Louise Woods for her hospitality. Shaking hands with Thorny Woods, the young engineer mounted and followed in LaSalle's wake.

Thorny Woods shrugged. "All loco, if yuh ask me," he said. "Now let's go fetch back some beef. Billy and Jake're awful slow 'bout it. I'll want twenty men, anyways."

Wayne Morgan slipped away, in the confusion as men saddled, checked their guns, mounted and rode out with Thorny Woods on the trail the two missing waddies had taken. He saddled Blue Hawk's gray and followed a short distance behind, as though accompanying the forage party, but once in the chaparral, he paused and signaled his Yaqui friend.

Blue Hawk appeared from a small side trail, leading Midnight. Swiftly Morgan changed to the black clothes, and tied the black domino mask across his rugged face.

"How far south is the sheriff?" he asked, as he settled his guns in their supple, oiled holsters.

"A mile, Senor."

"They killed both cowboys?"

Blue Hawk nodded, somberly. He mounted the gray and galloped on in the Masked Rider's wake. Ten minutes later they heard a sudden burst of heavy firing, and the shouts of men.

Along the side trail sped the man on the great black stallion. The powerful Midnight swerved west, breaking into the brush toward two lines of dismounted gunmen, Grole's bunch, who had surrounded Thorny Woods and his followers. Six-shooters and Winchesters barked death, men yelling in the fury of battle.

"The Masked Rider — here he comes!" That was Grole, howling the warning to his men.

The black-clad hombre's two heavy six-shooters spat into the killers' ranks. Accurate, cool aim knocked the gunnies off balance, tore the line. Charging on through the clearing where the ambush had been sprung, the Masked Rider drove the murderous deputies back, rolling them up into a frightened, screaming mass. His hot lead ripped into palpitating flesh. On the other side of the trail were more of Grole's killers, but the ranchers engaged them, protecting themselves, heartened by the example set by the cool-headed, fighting outlaw.

New hope sprang into the hearts of

Thorny Woods and his friends. They had all heard of the Masked Rider, of his sympathy toward the oppressed, the help he gave freely, without hope of return.

"That's the Masked Rider," bawled Woods. "He saved the Gregorys, boys, and now he's come to give us a hand!"

They swung their guns on the blazing array of weapons barking death into their ranks. Half a dozen waddies had gone down in the first awful volleys. Bullets crackled through the chaparral, dug up spurts of dirt. A horse screamed shrilly from a crippling slug.

The terrific attack launched by the Masked Rider smashed a way of retreat for Thorny Woods and his boys. They swung, spurring up out of the death trap, as Morgan's heavy guns picked off gunman after gunman who strove to stop them.

Thorny Woods, straight as a ramrod in his saddle despite his years, was last from the little clearing, herding his friends before him. A slug had pierced his left arm, another had cut a bloody groove in his seamed old cheek, and his clothes and Stetson were well ventilated, but he showed no signs of weakening.

"Thanks, Mr. Masked Rider," he roared, over the booming guns. "Yuh're welcome in

47

these parts — and my ranch is yores."

The howling, infuriated deputies, balked of their prey again by the Masked Rider, were unscrambling themselves and running on foot after their enemies. The Masked Rider emptied his Colts at them, and whirling, dashed away into the chaparral as Thorny Woods safely made the turn and galloped homeward.

Fifty feet from the south trail, Morgan, busily reloading his guns, suddenly saw Sheriff Grole and a dozen men spring up from the side. A leer of triumph exposed the sheriff's dirty teeth.

He had hustled back with his picked gunnies to catch the Masked Rider in his retreat — and it looked as though he was successful.

From the other side of the trail a Winchester suddenly barked. The man in front of Grole keeled over with a shriek, clutching at his punctured breast. Grole fired at the same instant that he ducked, startled by the whirl of another rifle slug. His bullet grazed the black-clad outlaw's cheek, nipping like a giant hornet, leaving a trail of blood. But for Blue Hawk's quick shots, Grole might have had the Masked Rider for whose scalp he so thirsted and whose hide was worth thousands of dollars.

The instant of opportunity passed. The black stallion crashed through the brush wall, and turning in his saddle, Morgan fanned his fresh-loaded guns at the bunched deputies. Grole stayed down behind the bodies of his gunnies, and Blue Hawk, leaping on his gray horse, escaped from the other side.

Contacting his Yaqui comrade later, east of the ambush spot, the Masked Rider said, "Blue Hawk, we're headin' for the Ruby Hills. Two engineers, from different mining companies, with their assayers, stopped at the Rabbit Leg this morning. They're after something up there, and I want to find what it is."

Blue Hawk nodded; he was ready to accept his friend's orders without question.

"More killers come to sheriff, Senor," was all he said.

"Yeah, they mean business. I suppose Grole'll attack the Rabbit Leg when he's got enough gunmen with him. I want to savvy why he's so anxious to put these poor ranchers off their land."

They started north along one of the narrow, winding cattle trails of the bush. A sudden "pop" right ahead told the Masked Rider a steer had taken to the chaparral. Pausing, he heard the crashing sounds as several cows broke through the thorny growth.

"Let's get 'em, Midnight," he murmured.

The black stallion cut up a side trail, while Blue Hawk waited. The Masked Rider got around to the other side of the small bunch of beeves, and started them back toward the Yaqui, riding on their tails at breakneck speed.

Blue Hawk turned them north and the two pushed the cows within sight of the Rabbit Leg corrals, urged them toward the ranch. Thorny Woods and his men had reached home, and a bunch now rode out to encircle the steers and rope them.

The Masked Rider waved his hand to them, and headed for the east-and-west trail on the north, the route to the Ruby Hills.

Blue Hawk had taken a roundabout course through the bush, and the two joined above the ranch and took the trail west.

Soon the road began to mount into the foothills. Red rocks stuck up, breaking the monotony of the chaparral ocean.

Now and then, gazing through a clear area, they could look up at the wooded mountains. Smoke rose in a thin column from near the summit of the largest peak.

"That'll be the spot Harrison and LaSalle are racin' to reach," decided the Masked

Rider, his eyes seeking the distant goal.

The way grew steeper, rockier. It was not a trail the black-clad outlaw fancied, for it offered too many chances of ambush, with its nests of rocks behind which armed men might hide to cover the trail.

He rode carefully, alert, watching the black stallion's ears for warning signals.

They climbed a steep slope, the north side dropping off sheer for a hundred feet, and the worn clay track swung to the left around a blood-red butte which towered over them. Midnight's hoofs dug in for a hold on the sliding footing.

The Masked Rider was well in advance of his Yaqui companion when Midnight's ears suddenly flattened out, then flicked erect. He gave a warning sniff, and the Masked Rider, as he reached for a six-gun, ducked down in the nick of time, for a bullet whirled within inches of the high, black Stetson crown. The crack of the rifle came from behind the red butte and the answering slug sent from Morgan's big Colt revolver spat leaden fragments into the eyes of the unseen drygulcher.

CHAPTER V
KING OF THE CAMP

Harrison, the young engineer, had paused only for snatches of sleep in his flying trip from Chicago to the Ruby Hills. He had been urged on by the exciting reports David Rose, the best assayer in the game, had made regarding the ore samples sent to the powerful Chicago Mining Corporation.

Advance agent for the C. M. C., with Rose along to check over the deposits from which the samples had come, Harrison had the authority to take an option. As he had been extremely successful during his meteoric career, the company would follow his advice in regard to purchase, checked by Rose's scientific skill in assaying.

"Looks as though the Arizona bunch will beat us to it, Rose," the young engineer remarked, as they pushed their horses west toward the mountains. "If the mine comes up to the specimen sent us it'll be the biggest yet."

David Rose was worn out from the rush to the Ruby Hills; he did not enjoy the wild land and the discomforts of field work, but it was part of his work and he bore it as well as he could.

"It'll be too bad if this LaSalle or whatever his name is takes an option," he commented. "If he's got any sense he'll buy one that'll hold until his assayer reports. Looks to me as though we've made a wild goose chase. I'm so sore from this constant riding I'm ready to quit. I wonder where the water would come from up here? It seems like pretty dry country."

The stalwart engineer's expert eye had already taken in the contours of the land as they mounted higher into the hills from which he could look back over the chaparral and see the range in perspective.

"The streams watering it come from these mountains. There would have to be a dam built to furnish enough water for wholesale refining."

"Yes, and I suppose once the news leaks out, there'll be a mad rush for the whole section. Those creeks would have washed down a good deal of loose stuff."

The lathered horses, bleeding from thorn scratches which they had received as the engineers shoved along the winding narrow trails from the town of Mescal where the coach from the Rio Grande and El Paso Railroad had dumped them, were straining against their straps as they climbed the rocky way, rounding a red butte. Rose shivered as he peeked over the edge of the precipice to their right; he instinctively drew his horse to the other side of the trail.

"Where yuh headin', Mister?" The hail came from behind the red butte, and a bearded face stared down at them.

The miner, whom Harrison decided was a lookout for the company in the Ruby Hills, blinked as he listened to the young engineer's explanation.

"Go ahead, Mister," the bearded hombre said. "You'll find Jake Worrell in charge." He gave three shrill whistles which echoed through the hills, obviously a signal.

"Did a slim man come up here with a big light-haired Swede?" asked Harrison anxiously. "They weren't far ahead of us."

"Haven't seen 'em," replied the trail guard. "I got orders to keep strangers out, 'cept if they got bus'ness with Lobster Jake."

"Queer," murmured Harrison. He hadn't, now he came to think on it, noticed any suspended dust in the past few miles, as he had after first leaving the Rabbit Leg Ranch. "That was a pretty girl," he thought, as he remembered Louise Woods. He felt guilty, for he had tarried longer than he should have merely to chat with the young woman. "Maybe LaSalle and the Swede got lost," Rose suggested, as they swung around the butte and walked their horses down across a dip, the bottom of which was paved with red, sliding shale.

"I don't see how they could manage to do that."

Up a pine-forested slope, they climbed until the great red cliffs seemed towering over them. A spring of clear water gushed from a black crevice and in the sheltered theater under the cliffs stood the mining camp. It consisted of tents and roughly built brush-and-rock shelters.

A few men were busy around the camp; a couple were preparing food, skinning a scrawny cow caught below in a grassy hollow, outside the cook shack. In the warm air the sound of picks and drills being hit with sledges rang metallically from the recesses of the mountain top. The camp was hard at work.

Rose and Harrison dismounted; they looked around for signs of LaSalle and Oley King. Paraphernalia familiar enough to the engineers — drills and hammers, rockers and pans, shovels and picks — and the necessary equipment for feeding and housing workers, stood here.

"Is Jake Worrell about?" Harrison inquired of a man working on the beef.

"Yeah, yonder he comes now, Mister," was the answer. Like the others in sight, the speaker wore corduroy pants tucked into miner's boots, a flannel khaki shirt, a felt hat.

Harrison swung as he heard a stone roll under an approaching man's boots. Lobster Jake Worrell was not tall but he had shoulders wide as a barn door and brawny arms with the muscles swelling them out in bow form. Heavy through the waist, his short legs seemed as sturdy as pine trunks. He had on high-laced brown shoes, worn army pants, and a brown flannel shirt. He did not wear any hat, and his brick hair matted and curled on his square head. He had a short mustache and there was a two-day beard stubble on his jutting chin.

Until Worrell spoke, Harrison thought he must be angry about something, for the skin of his cheeks and forehead was as red as a boiled lobster. But the wide-set, heavy-voiced camp boss was not in a temper at all: it was simply the way his skin reacted to sunlight, and Lobster Jake's flaming appearance never changed.

"Howdy, gents," Worrell said, holding out a stubby hand flecked with reddish hairs and covered with scars, cuts received during his work in the rocks and handling heavy tools.

He was, despite his excitable look and reddish coloring, a phlegmatic person — at least he seemed so to Harrison and Rose. The grip of his square-ended fingers was like a closing vise.

Bob Harrison smiled, drew forth his official card. Lobster Jake's red brow wrinkled up with the strain of reading it.

"Chicago, huh," he said, voice a deep rumble in the barrel chest. "There's plenty liquor and grub if you want it, gents. Make yoreselves to home."

"Your samples interested my company," explained Harrison pleasantly.

"Have you sold any option yet?"

"Nope, yuh're fust in, Harrison."

"Have you seen anything of a man named LaSalle?"

Lobster Jake shrugged; his head becoming almost neckless between the swelling muscles of his shoulders. "We've kept this purty quiet," he explained. "Don't want a lot of crazy fellers rushin' up here 'fore we're ready. Like to develop it ourselves on'y it would cost too much to build the plant needed. Got to have capital."

Harrison nodded. From Lobster Jake's remarks it was obvious the stocky man understood his work and was a veteran at it. The secrecy was to be commended. What had happened to prevent Albert LaSalle, his rival, from reaching the camp before him and taking first pick, was a mystery Harrison did not worry over, for it was a boon to him.

After a drink and a smoke, Harrison and Rose followed Lobster Jake up a beaten path, around the cliffs. There was a shaft cut into the mountainside, and a man with a rifle sat on guard at the entrance.

"We got to keep a sharp watch, so's we won't be rushed," Lobster Jake explained. He nodded to the sentinel who went on chewing his cud of tobacco as the three entered the shaft.

The sound of the picks and drills rang loud in their ears as they entered. Miners were at work, by the light of flaring torches, in the bowels of the mountain. The shaft ran a hundred feet straight in, then veered sharply to the south, and in a chamber that spread before them they saw the dark figures of the workers. Barrows of broken quartz ore stood about, ready to be pushed out. Harrison saw the efficient shoring, knew for certain that Lobster Jake was acquainted with his business.

By the reddish glow of the torches which made the air smoky and the eyes water — an up-and-down airshaft in the cliff created a draught that made breathing possible — Bob Harrison regarded the wide veins of yellow metal in the walls. David Rose was keenly examining the veins of the great gold mine.

After a preliminary survey, the three returned to Worrell's office. Harrison glanced inquiringly at Rose, who nodded and remarked succinctly:

"It looks good."

They were interrupted by the sound of shots. They went quickly outside, and heard heavy firing banged to the east.

"Hey, boys — hustle down and see what ails Mike," roared Lobster Jake.

Armed men dropped what they were doing and went running down toward the butte.

"This country's lousy with outlaws," growled Worrell, swinging back to Harrison and the assayer. "We've had a lot of trouble with 'em and with nosy fellers tryin' to git up and see what we're doin'. That's why we keep a guard."

"I'm authorized to take an option on the

mine, Worrell," Bob Harrison began, when they were once more settled inside. "Then Rose will make a more careful assay while I survey the country to see about development, water rights and so on."

Lobster Jake nodded, shrugged his great shoulders with his characteristic gesture. "I kin let yuh have a week's option. Hafta talk with my pardners in town 'bout the final sale."

"What d'you want down?"

"Oh, anything yuh say. Copla thousand be all right?"

Harrison nodded; it was cheap at the price. Next his skin he carried money belts containing three thousand dollars in large bills, and Rose had more. He paid over the two thousand, and Lobster Jake Worrell and he affixed their signature to an option form Harrison had with him.

The office was a one-room brush shack with Jake's bunk at the side, a table made of pine slabs; boxes served as chairs. Worrell shoved over a bottle of whiskey and tobacco.

The ink was hardly dry on the option paper when shouts rang out below. The shooting had ceased.

"Now what the hell's that?" growled Lobster Jake, stepping outside.

Harrison and Rose followed, stared down

the slope. The men who had hurried to help the trail guard were coming back across the shale, carrying the bearded fellow who had been on watch behind the red butte. And staggering along with them came two more dudes.

"Hello, here's LaSalle and King," Harrison said to Rose. "They look as though they'd been beaten up!"

Night was at hand, the hills bathed in the ruby glow of the fast-dropping sun. The miners were coming from the shaft, to eat and rest. Red fires were lit against the chill of the mountain darkness, for cooking. The men wore heavy boots to protect them against sharp rocks and the rattlesnakes which teemed in the wild fastnesses; corduroy pants, flannel shirts, caps or battered felts. Few took the trouble to shave so far from civilization, and a variety of beards decorated the stolid faces which were smeared with red dust and clay. Many wore guns in their wide leather belts.

Albert LaSalle's slender figure struggled up the slope into camp.

"Are you Jake Worrell?" he cried, breath coming in gasps. "I represent the Arizona Syndicate. We're interested in your proposition, and I'm ready to take an option —"

He saw Bob Harrison then, standing near

the office, and broke off, frowning angrily. The big Swede lumbered up behind his friend. Oley King's clothing, like LaSalle's, was badly torn and smeared with dirt. Both men seemed exhausted.

"Sorry, but this gent from the east beat yuh up here," drawled Lobster Jake, shrugging.

LaSalle's eyes burned into Harrison's. He could not hold back his fury. His fists were clenched as he stepped past Lobster Jake and confronted the young engineer.

"You're damned smart, aren't you?" he shouted, shaking his fist in Harrison's face. "You think you've beaten me, but you haven't!"

"Take it easy, LaSalle," Harrison said calmly. "It's all a matter of business. The first one in gets the first choice."

The Arizona Syndicate engineer was almost beside himself with a rage Harrison could not understand. He himself had been beaten to strikes, but he had never let it upset him this way.

"You can't make a fool out of me," raged LaSalle, following as Harrison stepped back. "Do you think I don't realize *you* arranged the holdup that kept me from getting up here first, Harrison?"

"What?" gasped Harrison. He didn't

understand for a moment what LaSalle was driving at. "What holdup?"

"What holdup!" sneered LaSalle. "Half a dozen bandits — fake bandits — jumped out of the bush while we were on our way here and captured King and me. They robbed us, stole our horses, and set us afoot miles from the road! I know you hired them to prevent me beating you to the mine."

"That's a crazy lie!" cried Harrison hotly.

CHAPTER VI
HORNET'S NEST

The infuriated LaSalle leaped at him, striking at his face. Harrison deftly caught the slim man's wrist, turning him aside so that he lost his balance and fell heavily to the ground.

The big Swede, Oley King, growled ominously in his throat. He lunged in, like a grizzly bear, seized Harrison around the waist as the other turned away from LaSalle.

"You ban hit my boss," rumbled King, "I break you in two."

The pressure of the assayer's mighty arms squeezed all the breath from Harrison's lungs. Then he braced himself, digging in his boot heels as he grappled to keep King from bearing him to the earth. For a minute the two powerful young men strained against one another silently, only the sound of their constrained breath coming from them. Harrison could just about hold his own against the big Swede.

Then Lobster Jake Worrell, with a muttered curse, jumped in, grasped King's wrist and broke his grip on the panting Harrison. The boss of the camp knew all the tricks of rough and tumble fighting, and with a quick twist he turned the Swede and sent him, with a knee in the back, staggering away.

"Cut it out," Lobster Jake ordered. "Leave him be, both of yuh."

King scowled, but did not come back to the attack. The onlookers gave a sigh of disgust; it would have been a good fight if the strong men had really fought it out.

"Say, Jake," reported one of them from the butte, "look. Mike's got a crease through the hair that knocked him silly. When we got down he was jist foldin' up, and we seen a feller on a black hoss, his face masked, and wearin' a black cape, turnin' off down the trail. Shot at him but he give us the slip and escaped."

Jake Worrell swore hotly. "All in black — say, I'll bet that's the Masked Rider outlaw I've heard tell of! We'll need to keep a sharp watch, boys. He may be meanin' to rob our camp."

Bob Harrison, disgusted at LaSalle's actions, knowing himself to be innocent of the holdup which the Arizona Syndicate's representative claimed had delayed him, swung on his heel, leaving the furious La-Salle to pick himself up. He was weary, and needed sleep.

Lobster Jake grinned at him, winked, muttered, "Right salty, ain't he? Never mind, yuh got the option, Harrison." Then Worrell led the C. M. C. men to a tent with two bunks in it where they might sleep.

It did not take Harrison long to fall into a deep unconsciousness; he didn't even hear Rose get into his bed.

While the camp slept, silent save for an occasional thud of a rifle butt on a rock as a sentry rested his gun, men were meeting in a hidden gulch below.

The silver moon shone bright in the wilderness sky, but up under the steep cliff, shadows were black as pitch.

"Listen, Flynn, I ain't bin able to take over the Rabbit Leg yit," the harsh voice of Sheriff Grole reported. "Thorny Woods was ready for us and he's got fifty to sixty fightin' men collected there. They stood us off."

"Fool," said Flynn coldly. "You must finish 'em off within the next twenty-four hours. Go back and attack them — burn the place if you have to!"

"Figger we'll need them deeds right soon, Chief," a third man announced.

From the way the two addressed the man called Flynn, with mingled fear and politeness, it was obvious he was in full command, the leading evil spirit of all. He seemed to emanate a devilish power, a raw, murderous aura that awed even such lawless spirits as Pat Grole.

"Everything's okay at your end, Jake?" Vernon Flynn demanded. "He's taken the bait?"

"Yessir, swallered it hook, line and sinker. All's fine."

"H'm. I wish Grole could say the same," Flynn remarked sarcastically.

"Aw, Flynn, I got a lot of the ranches, ain't I? And I'll git the Rabbit Leg, too. I got more men comin' in and the ones yuh sent for from acrost the Rio're pullin' in. Bandits from all along the Border've heard we kin use 'em, and with their guns we kin easy win."

"Yes, yes," Flynn growled impatiently, "I worked it all out, Grole, so I know what's going on. I've timed the whole play to the second, too, and I don't want any fool bungling it, savvy? I saw Ike Norton before I left Mescal and he's handled his end well. He's filed the Rabbit Leg with the rest, and that ought to fill out all of the range we've got to have."

"If it hadn't bin for that sidewinder of an outlaw," explained Grole aggrievedly, "I'd of finished up Thorny Woods today. I'll hang that Masked Rider's hide on my corral fence 'fore I'm through."

"What's that? There's someone up there!" Flynn's hissed alarm froze them an instant; then hands flew to six-shooters, leather holsters scratching as the guns emerged. The clicks of cocked triggers were sharply audible in the night.

Against the moonsky, above them on the bushed edge of the gulch, framed for an instant on the silver background, showed a magnificent horseman. On the back of the giant black stallion sat a black-cloaked figure, the paler tint of the rugged jaw dully visible under the domino mask.

"That's him — that's the Masked Rider," bawled Sheriff Grole, throwing up his gun and lifting his thumb off the hammer.

Guns crashed heavily in the darkness. The black stallion leaped high as the Masked Rider's pistols roared in reply to the men in the gulch. The three below, fearful for their lives in the face of this terrific blast, fell face down in the jagged rocks. Bullets rapped about them and none of the trio dared raise his head until the Masked Rider's guns fell silent, and a bunch of hustling gunmen,

Grole's "deputies," came yelling and clattering in from the trail where they had been awaiting their master.

"Git him — he's up there, boys!" shrieked the frantic Grole.

They glimpsed the horseman above, and dozens of gun muzzles swung to cover the mysterious bandit. But an instant before the deadly fusillade rapped out to tear chunks from the cliff lip and whistle in the air, the Masked Rider faded back.

He heard the bullets of hatred whirling about him, felt the burn of a close one along his forearm, and the violent twitch of his black sombrero as another ventilated the high crown.

"Back, Midnight," he urged.

He hastily reloaded his hot Colts. The savagery of the enemies he fought, many of them as yet unmarked to him, did not force him into retreat; instead it made him burn with a reciprocal anger, and his strong jaw was set as he looked back toward the gulch.

The fact that the trail sentry that afternoon, as the black-clad hombre appeared on his way to the mountain camp of Lobster Jake, had fired upon him, had not greatly surprised Morgan; he was used to having men's guns against him. People were greedy for the reward money posted, ready to be

69

paid to any gunfighter without question who would fetch in the Masked Rider's scalp.

He had creased the sentry, shoved back down the trail and faded into the brush. Warning Blue Hawk as the Yaqui approached, he had decided to wait till dark before approaching the mountain encampment.

They had napped for a time. The night had been well along when they rose and ate a cold snack.

"Hafta work to the south to git past that butte," the Masked Rider had said.

It had been hard going, for the slopes grew much steeper, but they had moved carefully, slowly, weaving up through pine forests and dense brush covering the mountains. Sometimes, when faced by an impassable cliff, they had been forced to go back and start over again from another angle.

Then Blue Hawk had warned, "Someone over there, Senor," and had waved toward the trail.

Working back, the Masked Rider heard the click of stones under hoofs. He had found the gulch which opened off the road to the mountain encampment, and, as he silently came up to the brink of the ravine, he caught the low voices of men below. This conference had aroused his suspicion, but before he could catch what was being said by these mysterious conspirators, the keen-eyed Flynn had glimpsed him and given the alarm.

Morgan heard Sheriff Grole calling upon his gunmen and recognized the officer's voice.

Thus, this present skirmish had begun. As he retreated, Blue Hawk came to join him. Midnight found a way across the rough ground, from the lip of the gulch. But the sheriff's hombres were slow scrambling up the steep rock walls of the ravine. By the time they made it, the Masked Rider and the Yaqui were half a mile south of the gulch.

"You go on, Senor?" inquired Blue Hawk.

"Shore, more so than ever. If Grole came all the way up here it must have been to report to somebody. I reckon there's a hookup between the sheriff and that mining camp, Blue Hawk. And I've got to find out what it is."

Feeling a way with the expert Indian tracker's assistance, the Masked Rider finally got up to the summit south of Lobster Jake's camp. Dismounting, he left Midnight with Blue Hawk and the gray — for the climb down to the dark mouth of the shaft, which he could just see below, was far too precipitous for a horse to negoti-

71

ate. Shucking his spurs, which would catch on the rocks and impede him, the black-clad hombre began to descend a red rock wall by means of the small ledges which afforded hand- and foot-holds.

Keeping in the shadows as far as possible, with the red glow of the camp-fires to the north, he reached the bush-covered bottom below the hill and, a wraith in the moonlight, approached the mouth of the mine.

He paused to listen, peering at the pitch-black adit. It seemed utterly deserted, and he heard nothing from the camp. He stepped closer to the hole in the side of the hill. Still he was not challenged, and he quickly went inside.

As he disappeared from the moonlight, a shotgun barrel was rammed into his back ribs and a gruff voice snarled:

"Got yuh! Throw up yore hands, or I'll blow yore liver out!"

The guard had been standing just inside the pitch-black entrance. He had let the spying stranger come in, and now had him pinned with death. Morgan could not even see his enemy, for the man was behind him, but he could feel the nudging double barrels of the murderous shotgun, however, and he knew that the slightest error on his part

72

would mean horrible and sudden annihilation.

The great wads and many shot would blow him wide open. He raised his hands quickly.

"Turn round, slow," ordered his captor, "and march — pronto, now."

The Masked Rider obeyed. He walked carefully ahead, urged on by the shotgun.

"Where yuh takin' me?" he drawled.

"Shut up, outlaw! Lobster Jake'll shore be glad to see yuh. He'll give me plenty fer this." The miner was plainly delighted with himself at capturing the famous bandit. "Tryin' to sneak in and steal our gold, huh? Jake'll teach yuh, damn yore dirty hide!"

The Masked Rider walked, hands high as slowly as he dared. The miner's trigger finger was itching; it was only that he wanted the pleasure of walking the famous outlaw into camp alive that he had not already killed his captive. Morgan watched for a chance, just the slightest break so that he might drop and whirl. He was determined to risk death rather than be taken to Lobster Jake, this hombre's boss. But the man who had him was an expert with guns and wary, evidently picked just for those qualifications.

They came to the turn, where the path

from the gold mine swung around and into the flat area in which the camp was pitched. The reddish glow of the fires showed the settlement to the eyes of the Masked Rider. He quickly took in the huts and tents, the paraphernalia of the mining camp. There were men with rifles lounging about, and as the spot came into full view, Morgan saw a squat, extremely broad man walking in from the trail that led below.

"Hey, Jake," sang out his captor. "Look what I got for yuh. It's the Masked Rider."

Lobster Jake jerked around, his red face turning toward the approaching men. With a curse he whipped out a pistol and lumbered across the clearing as shouting men jumped up to follow him.

Wayne Morgan drew in a deep breath. Now was the moment to act. He must escape now or it would be too late.

He would pretend to stumble, fall, whirling as he went down, on the narrow chance that the miner would hold his fire an instant, a precious instant that would allow one of the heavy Colts to come into action.

The night was suddenly rent, close at hand, by the terrible snarl of a mountain lion. It was so real that the Masked Rider was startled for a moment, eyes involuntarily turning up toward the steep red cliff from which the growls came.

The effect on the miner guard was magical.

"Cougar!" he screamed, leaping back.

Chapter VII
Mescal Town

Dropping from the cliff, twenty feet above, a lithe body flashed downward — not a lion, but Blue Hawk. The Yaqui had seen the Masked Rider emerge from the mine shaft as a prisoner with the gun in his back, and hurriedly working along the cliff with the agility of a mountain goat to a point just above, had launched himself to the rescue.

His cougar-like snarl had sent panic into the miner's heart for a second, diverting the shotgun from Morgan's vitals. At that, the Yaqui, with his single twelve-inch fang of steel, was far more dangerous than any wild beast.

"Hey — what the hell's that?" bawled Lobster Jake Worrell.

His men were rousing up, grabbing their guns, jumping after their boss. The guard with the shotgun had recovered and swung the double-barreled weapon upward. But his masked prisoner was already in action.

Whirling, the Robin Hood outlaw drove his fist squarely into the guard's face, a lashing, hard blow that turned the shotgun inches off its course. The heavy concentrated slugs from the two barrels whooshed with a horrid sound past Blue Hawk's hurtling figure. A second-fraction later the lithe Indian landed on the husky miner, and the sharp blade pressed to the man's throat as he fell, unconscious.

Blue Hawk's knees rested on the miner's chest, his leap cushioned by the unfortunate fellow. The Masked Rider drew a gun to answer shots that came from Lobster Jake and his oncoming crew. A slug bit at Morgan's cheek, another tore a chunk from his boot.

"Shall I keel, Senor?" growled Blue Hawk, the knife against the throat of the prostrate miner. A thin red line showed where the biting, keen blade had cut the surface skin.

"No — come on," ordered the Masked Rider, deciding quickly.

He fired over the heads of the attacking miners, close shots that tipped their hats and then others that whipped up puffs of dirt at their feet. The runners grew less eager to reach the rock turn. The black-clad outlaw shoved Blue Hawk ahead of him and fled out of sight of Lobster Jake and his men.

They hurried up the narrow cut. Passing the black mine mouth, they reached the spot where they might climb on up to the spot where they had left their horses. Lobster Jake and his men, heavily armed, had slowed down to make the blind turn where their suddenly silenced guard lay on the rocky ground. They burst into view as the Yaqui went up the cliff like a climbing monkey, the Masked Rider at his heels, a gun ready in one hand.

"There they go — I see 'em," bellowed Lobster Jake.

A bullet hit the eroded cliffside, ricocheted between Blue Hawk and his beloved Senor. The Masked Rider paused to shoot back, to slow down the pursuit. A bulge of rock protected them from the direct fire for precious moments, then Blue Hawk pulled himself up to the top and began to fire his rifle at the flashes from the miners.

The Robin Hood outlaw crawled over the top, and the two men hurried to the gray and Midnight. Mounting, they began to make their way back down the mountain.

"Where now, Senor?" asked Blue Hawk. "You find what you wish?"

The other nodded somberly. "It's gold,

Blue Hawk. And I reckon Jim Woods oughta know pronto. A big strike in the Ruby Hills makes this range very valu'ble, and that may explain why Grole and his friends want the land."

Behind them they heard the angry roars of the baffled Lobster Jake, and his tough cronies. The Masked Rider knew that the secret meeting he had run on below the camp, proved a connection between Sheriff Grole and the red-faced king of the gold miners.

"Wonder who that third hombre was? Seemed like a big boss," he mused.

Inwardly he swore to stand between the brutal armies of Grole and Lobster Jake, and Thorny Woods' simple, honest ranchers. Alone save for Blue Hawk, again the Masked Rider was making a play for the right, to save innocent victims from oppression and death forced on them by killers who were completely maddened by greed.

Grayness showed in the sky ahead as they cautiously picked a way toward the Rabbit Leg. They were traveling a winding, small trail which was nearly parallel with the main east-west road when, from a slight elevation, they could look down and see the outlines of the ranch buildings.

Swiftly changing into his Wayne Morgan

garb, the Masked Rider exchanged horses with Blue Hawk and carefully approached the ranch. He was sure that Grole would have men watching the trails, and he was ready when he heard the rustle of brush to the right, at a sharp bend, and a man with a Winchester rifle in his hands jumped out to stop him.

"Hey, you," the trail sentry growled, "git off that gray hoss and —" The rifle barrel was rising to cover the wandering waddy.

But even as the gun muzzle came up toward his heart, Wayne Morgan's heavy six-shooter appeared as though by magic. The rifleman gasped in fright at the terrible, efficient speed of that draw, and pulled the Winchester trigger too soon. The slug whistled wildly past the neck of the gray as Morgan's gun roared. He fell back, hitting the brush wall, smashing it down with his body, knocked over by the force of Morgan's bullet which blasted out his evil life.

Blue Hawk swept into sight ready with his rifle to help his leader. But he wasn't needed; Morgan already was riding on. He soon reached the Rabbit Leg clearing, singing out so the guards would not fire on him.

Shorty hurried across the yard, to greet him. "Howdy, waddy. Where the hell'd yuh git to? We missed yuh."

"Figgered that sheriff feller might git too close," Morgan told him, keeping to the character the ranchers had pinned on him when he first appeared. "Bin layin' out in the bush. Where's yore boss?"

"Thorny? Oh — he ain't here jist now." Shorty's tone was evasive and he changed the subject, "C'mon in and git some grub. Yuh wanta watch how yuh ride these trails, yuh're likely to git a bullet in the craw. You fire them shots jist now?"

Morgan nodded. "Yeah," he drawled. "Kilt a snake."

Abreast the front porch, Morgan saw armed ranchers lying around waiting to defend the ranch from an attack by Grole.

Louise Woods was on the verandah and she called out.

"Shorty — have you found out what those shots were? I'm worried sick about Grand-father; I'm afraid he'll never get to Mescal."

"So that's it," thought Morgan.

"It's this Morgan feller come back. He fired at a rattler," Shorty told Louise cheer-fully.

The girl gave Morgan a faint smile of welcome, a troubled line between her eyes. Shorty led him to the cook shack talking in a low voice.

"Now yuh know where the old man went

to. Him and sev'ral ranchers done rode to Mescal to see what's goin' on at the county seat, and to complain 'bout Grole.

"They rode out durin' the night?" inquired Morgan.

"Yeah, that's it. Yuh won't tell nobuddy, will yuh?"

Shorty was watching him narrowly. The cowboy was pretty sure this Morgan fellow was a friend, but suspicion was running high in the chaparral. Grole had enlisted and brought in killer-gunmen, giving them free rein to rob and slay in return for their services.

" 'Course not; yuh kin count on me, Shorty," Morgan assured him solemnly.

"Thank yuh."

"I hope Woods gits to town," Morgan went on. "Grole's shore coverin' the trails. That was a human snake I shot, Shorty; one of Grole's hombres."

Shorty's eyes widened; then he shrugged. "The boss knows these trails like a book. He'll git through, I'm bettin' on it."

An hour later Wayne Morgan quietly slipped away from the Rabbit Leg, bound for Mescal town.

Mescal stood along the western bank of Webb Creek which was a brown sandy-bottomed tributary of the Nueces. When it rained the creek rose and sometimes flooded Main Street, which thoroughfare was deeply rutted by wagon wheels. When the sun dried out the earth, it powdered into dust that billowed up in choking clouds around the beating hoofs of horses.

The chaparral had been cleared for some distance around the town. The plaza was a bare, windswept area splitting the main road which crossed Webb Creek past the town and continued eastward.

There were saloons and stores to supply the outlying ranches with amusement and necessities.

The chief architectural feature of Mescal was the City Hall, standing on a slight hill to the south of the plaza. It was made of adobe brick, three feet thick, and topped with a parapet roof — a fort-like structure which served to hold the county records, the jail, and sheriff's quarters.

The place was referred to by the inhabitants as the "Fort." Originally it had been just that, a protection in the old days against Indian and Mexican raiders who had long considered all territory south of the Nueces their stamping grounds.

The gentle night wind, aromatic with the chaparral scent, whirled up little clouds of red dust on the plaza and road as Wayne

Morgan dismounted to look the town over. He had struck the main trail a mile east of the Rabbit Leg, and ridden it through to Mescal. Forced to make a run for it when he bumped into a patrol of Grole's gunnies, he had a fresh crease in the flesh of his left thigh where one of their slugs had burnt him. He limped slightly as he led the gray into the livery stable and handed over a dollar to the wrangler, for a grain feed and rub-down.

Lights were already on in the saloons, and in the homes. The music from a honky-tonk piano sounded in the air. Stiff from long hours in the saddle, Wayne Morgan strolled under the wooden sun awnings built over the board walks, keeping out of the way of cowboys and townsmen.

It did not take him long to find Thorny Woods and his half dozen chaparral-scarred and grim-faced friends. They were sitting at a round table in a corner of the Red Queen saloon and gambling hall, drinking and talking earnestly in low tones.

Sawdust covered the floor of the big bar-room; a wide door opened into the gambling hall at the rear where black-clad, solemn men turned their cards. Along the bar stood cowboys and men in town garb, and in the back a derbied piano player kept the keys busy.

"Hello, Morgan," said Thorny Woods, evidently surprised but keeping it controlled as the wandering waddy halted at the table. "Sid down, and I'll buy yuh a drink. How'd yuh happen to come to this town?"

Woods obviously believed him a man on the dodge who wasn't apt to visit such a public spot as Mescal. Morgan sat down next to the old fellow, aware of suspicious eyes turning on him, for the ranchers were in that mood. They wouldn't talk of their affairs before a stranger, and while Morgan had shown himself a friend, Sheriff Grole had been using bush fugitives and outlaws against them.

"I went to yore ranch," Morgan told him, keeping his voice low, "huntin' yuh. I made the trip up to the Ruby Hills, and there's a gold mine up there. Dunno how big it is, but if it's any account it may make your range very valu'ble. They'll need water, mebbe a reservoir, and when the word leaks outside it'll mean a run this way. Yore land 'll fetch high prices."

"A gold mine!" exclaimed Woods unbelievingly. "Why, I own them hills; leastaways, I've run my cows in 'em fifty years! Never knowed there was gold up there."

"Gold's where yuh find it," remarked Wayne Morgan. "I didn't git to see the mine itself. A feller named Lobster Jake bosses the camp, and he's got a hundred tough miners up there. By the way they act, it's mighty rich and they're tryin' to keep strangers out, prob'ly till they git all set and have title to yore range."

Woods frowned, forehead deeply corrugated, his old face stern.

"So that's the game," he growled. "Yuh savvy, boys? Grole's in on this dirty game to rob us of our range."

"Gold!" cried a startled rancher, so loudly that everybody turned to look at him.

"Quiet, yuh danged fool," ordered Thorny Woods. "Yuh wanta tell the hull world 'bout it? It means our range'll be overrun with prospectors and strangers; there'll be an end to cattle ranchin' down here. I ain't interested in gittin' gold; it on'y brings misery. What I want is peace and my range."

"We kin sell out and buy land somewheres else," another rancher suggested.

Morgan shook his head. "Unless yore titles are clear, yuh can't sell. It's plain Grole's hooked into this. He knowed of this gold strike and that's why he's takin' yore range. But it must be deeper than Grole, seems to me; there's this new county formed, and that law 'bout registerin' within thutty days. It smells ratty. I reckon Grole's got somebuddy bossin' in, someone who thought this all up."

Thorny Woods banged a gnarled fist on the table so hard the glasses jumped and tinkled.

"Yuh're right, Morgan; yuh're a danged smart lad! C'mon, boys, let's go over to Ike Norton's house. His wife said he'd be home by nine o'clock, and it's most that now."

"Who's Norton?" Morgan asked, arising with the others.

"The County Commissioner — has charge of the land files in Chaparral," Woods explained. "We done rode here to see him but he wasn't in town today."

CHAPTER VIII
COURTHOUSE
RECORDS

Paying for their drinks, the eight men left the Red Queen strolling along the wooden walk together. At a lighted house near the north side they turned in, heavy boots thudding on the porch. Thorny Woods rapped on the door with a gun butt. After a moment a high-pitched voice answered from inside.

"Who's that?" it asked.

"Open up, Ike," ordered Woods. "It's Jim Woods. We wanta talk to yuh."

"Come round to the office in the morning," the high voice replied. "I ain't seein' nobody on business at night."

Morgan thought he sensed a quaver of fear in it.

Thorny Woods promptly responded by putting his shoulder against the door, and shoving.

The barrier burst inward sending a small, pale-faced man flying back against the wall.

Ike Norton was small and very thin, with a pasty, sharp face. He had a long, narrow nose and close-set black eyes set deep in his sparse-haired head. His hands were slender, with well kept nails and he rubbed one over the other nervously as he shrank before the grim old rancher chief.

"What you mean by forcin' your way in here like this?" he squeaked.

"Jist want a word with yuh, Ike," Woods told him easily. "We ain't goin' to harm yuh, yuh needn't be afraid. But we got to find out 'bout this land snatch. Yuh savvy what's goin' on?"

Ike Norton shrugged, took heart as he realized the cowmen were not going to attack him.

"Why, only what I've heard, Woods. My job is registerin' titles, and there have been a good deal of tranferrin' lately."

"And this here new law, that a man loses his land if he ain't registered in Chaparral County?"

"That's the rulin'," nodded Norton.

"Why wasn't we told of it?"

The County Commissioner shrugged. "It was posted, gents."

"Who's claimin' our range?"

"I'll hafta look it up, Woods. I got it all in the records at the Town Hall."

Thorny Woods, scowling, stuck out a brawny hand, gripped the front of Norton's black coat. "Git yore keys and we'll go over there now and find out."

"It's too late," objected Norton. "Come to my office at nine tomorrer mornin'."

Thorny Woods stuck out his chin. "You'll do it now, Ike. Git yore hat."

"Aw, right," whined Norton.

He found his hat and, walking ahead of the ranchers, strode across to the fortlike city hall. After unlocking the land office door, he struck a match and touched it to the wick of an oil lamp which stood on the desk. Files stood about, records of the new Chaparral County.

Slowly, under the prodding of Jim Woods, the County Commissioner began bringing forth records.

"Who's claimin' my range and the Ruby Hills?" demanded Woods.

Silently Norton showed him the record.

"Jacob Worrell," read Woods aloud.

"I know him; that'll be Lobster Jake, the boss of that minin' camp," Morgan told Woods.

For a half hour they searched the records, checking up the new claimants to their various lands. Sheriff Pat Grole had filed several claims, and there were others, names the cowmen did not know. But, as Morgan suggested, probably they were dummies, tools of Worrell and Grole. The name of Vernon Flynn, Morgan noted, was there with the others.

"It's a damn dirty steal!" growled Woods. His friends were furious inside, faces burning with anger. "They won't git way with it, boys, not while I kin handle a six-gun."

"Don't talk like a fool, Woods," quavered Norton. "You can't fight the law."

Suddenly Wayne Morgan whirled, hands flying to the six-shooters at his thighs. He had heard the stealthy tread of men out in the hallway. As he crouched down in front of the desk, watching the entrance, he saw Pat Grole leap into sight, pistols up to cover the men in the land office. The burly sheriff was backed by a number of his hard-faced, heavily armed men, his deputy gun fighters.

"Yuh fellers are under arrest," bawled Grole furiously. "I want yuh all for murder, shootin' my deputies —"

Thorny Woods swung, with an angry curse. His old eyes flashed blue sparks of defiance.

"Yuh're nuthin' but a danged dirty thief, Grole," he yelled, voice booming in the confined space of the office. "And I kin prove it. I'll —"

Ike Norton squeaked like the rat he was, fell flat behind the side of the oak desk. Grole's six-shooter glinted in the rays of the lamp as it swung to pin Jim Woods. Wayne Morgan saw the death threat in Grole's fierce eyes and fired hastily just as the sheriff's gun flamed. Thorny Woods staggered back against the wall, his mouth dropping open, eyes widening in dazed shock. A trickle of blood came from his white hair, ran down his brow and cheek, dripped from his chin to the floor. Then his knees gave way and he folded up on the boards.

Grole yipped with pain as his gun, the cylinder twisted by the impact of Morgan's slug, was violently wrenched from his grip. He doubled up, holding his stung, bruised hand with his left. "Git 'em — shoot 'em all down!" he shrieked, red rage flushing his hot brain.

Morgan's Colt barrel swept in a swift arc, cracked against the lamp on the desk, knocked it over. It crashed on the floor, instantly going out and plunging the office in darkness. "Down, ev'rybuddy," he shouted.

Deputies bunched in the doorway opened fire, their guns flashing red-yellow; bullets rapped into the thick 'dobe walls, and men howled in the excitement of battle.

Crouched low by the side of the thick oak desk, Wayne Morgan began shooting with his expert cadence and balanced aim at the gunmen. He nicked one man's ear, stung a second in the arm with a bullet, and perforated hats. Inside of two moments the doorway had cleared. None of Grole's hired gunnies cared to stand up there and die; and they could no longer see the ranchers inside the office.

Acrid powder smoke burned Morgan's flared nostrils as he swiftly sought a way out of the death trap. The windows all around the town hall were heavily barred with steel, like the jail itself. The main entry was clogged by Grole's murderous deputies. But he remembered he had noted a smaller, bolted portal at the rear of the land office.

It was Morgan's habit, hunted and harassed as he was, to take careful stock of such things. Gun in right hand, he slid swiftly along the wall, and felt with his left for the door. Finding it, he eased the bolt back with his supple fingers.

The fusillade booming in the big building had reached the ears of townfolk, men in the saloons and homes; people came hurrying to the place to see what went on, hundreds of citizens bunching up outside.

"This way, cowmen," Morgan called, voice

93

low but penetrating.

But the fall of their chief had paralyzed the ranchers; they were slow to answer, and precious seconds flew by. Wayne Morgan cursed under his breath; it was only a matter of seconds if they were to get out of there.

"Reckon I'd better git out and see what I can do then," he muttered. To allow himself to be taken with the cowmen would not help them any. He yanked open the little door.

"Hey — hustle back there and cut 'em off!" That was Sheriff Grole, seeing the rectangle of the hall light through the door Morgan had opened.

Bullets came through the other entry, at an angle, spanging into the wood, the mud walls, and kissing the fugitive's clothes with vicious caresses of death. The burn of one along his thigh sent him plunging aside, head-first, out of sight of Grole and his devilish crew.

He was in a narrow corridor which ran into the main hall at right angles; he ran on down this, with windows on his right hand, but all heavily barred with steel, offering no way out. There was no exit. He passed a flight of wooden stairs that evidently led up to the second story, and at the next turn, was greeted by howls and bullets as more of the sheriff's gang, who had run along the front of the building, cut him off.

Desperate, Wayne Morgan leaped back, his gun snarling defiance. He was close to the steps, as Grole's hombres from the other side appeared at the junction of the corridors, to kill him. Leaping up the stairs, boots cracking heavily on the creaking boards, he reached the second floor and jumped from sight as men appeared below. Bullets whined in his wake. The upper story was dark, but he could see the glows marking the windows — all of them barred.

He quickly struck a match, the little flame of light showing he was in a big chamber. There was a ladder in the room and his eyes sought the ceiling where the ladder led up to a trapdoor. He mounted swiftly, as his pursuers clattered up the stairs, shouting to him to surrender.

Shoving up the trapdoor, he pushed through the opening just as they entered the chamber. They glimpsed his disappearing boots, fired after him, but he slammed the trapdoor and ran to the parapet. The roof was flat, and he could see the glow of the town lights all around him. The yells of his excited enemies rang out below. The parapet was pierced by narrow slits through which defenders could fire their rifles and hold off attack.

Down below dark figures were running around to the back of the city hall to cut him off. It was now or never, and he seized the brief moment he had left to save himself.

On the night air the defiant howl of a mountain lion rang out, as Wayne Morgan let his lithe body down the outside of the parapet, hung by his hands, and then let go.

It was a long drop from the parapet to the earth, but Morgan knew how to fall. He let his knees buckle as he hit, rolling over and over on the sandy ground, relaxing his muscles and tendons, presenting fleshy portions of his body instead of bones that would break. The jolt took away his breath and he was badly bruised, but he came up on his knees, rose and scurried off toward the dark outline of a large stable behind the city hall.

"There he goes!" yelled a deputy, glimpsing the dark, running figure, and splinters flew from the corner of the wooden building, bullets whistling in the night air.

Morgan ducked to the other side, out of their sight. To the south he heard the answering cry of Blue Hawk, and swung that way. The white-clad Yaqui, dark hair bunched back by the red band, long knife gleaming in his colored sash, shoved Midnight to his side.

"Take him, Senor," ordered Blue Hawk, leaving the saddle in a single bound.

Breath rasping in and out of his powerful lungs, Wayne Morgan leaped into the saddle, clamping his iron legs against the black stallion's ribs.

"Yore gray's at the Crown Livery Corral," he told the Yaqui, who nodded, turned, and ran through an alley, where he could easily fade out of sight or mingle with the excited crowds in Mescal town.

The black stallion's flashing legs quickly took Morgan out of immediate danger. Safely away, he stopped and unrolled the pack at the cantle, finding his black cape and hat. He swiftly donned the Masked Rider clothes, and now, in his black outfit and domino mask, he was again the mysterious fugitive and Nemesis of the range.

Chin grimly set, gritted teeth gleaming beneath the black blur of the mask, he turned and rode back to face his foes.

"Hey — there's the Masked Rider!"

Pursuing deputies, after the waddy who had escaped their trap at the City Hall, brought up short, boots sliding in the dust as they saw the flashing, black-clad hombre charging at them. Wild bullets missed him by feet, as they lost their nerve and, turning tail, hustled back to the safety of the crowd.

But Sheriff Grole now had Thorny Woods and his friends, prisoners inside the thick walls of the Town Hall. Hundreds of people were massed around the structure, and the Masked Rider could not fight through such a mob without injuring decent citizens. He was blocked temporarily from any attempt to rescue the ranchers; and he did not know just how badly Woods was hurt. The old man might even be dead.

He reluctantly turned Midnight north and rode away into the bush, disappearing in the night and its shadows.

CHAPTER IX
RUNNING FIGHT

Safe at last, the Masked Rider dismounted and rolled himself a smoke. Squatting in the chaparral outside the town, he waited for the hubbub to die down. He rested an hour, reloading and checking his guns. Then he heard the low call of Blue Hawk, and answering, the Yaqui soon was at his side, riding the gray horse.

"So yuh got him," approved the Masked Rider, nodding at the animal.

"Si, Senor. Was easy."

Most Indians were expert horse thieves. Though Blue Hawk was honest, and the gray was theirs, he had enjoyed the little problem of taking the horse out from under the nose of the livery stable wrangler without the latter realizing anyone was near.

"What they doin' in town?" the white man asked.

"Big noise, Senor." Blue Hawk gave an expressive gesture, showing the excitement of the populace.

"Did Grole kill the ranchers?"

Blue Hawk shook his head. "Put in prison, Senor."

"Huh. I s'pose he didn't dare shoot 'em down in cold blood in front of so many witnesses. But he'll finish 'em as soon as he kin." The Robin Hood outlaw arose, tall body straightening.

"Where you go, Senor?"

"They oughta quiet down soon, Blue Hawk. And — well, I've gotta get those men out of there, before Grole murders 'em."

Slowly the two rode back toward the glow of Mescal town. From the dark bush outskirts to the west, they could look out and see the wind-swept, bare plaza and the front of the city hall. The adobe fort was ringed by armed hombres, Grole's killers.

"There's the Sheriff — and Norton," muttered the Masked Rider, as the two emerged from the front door of the hall and crossed the corner of the plaza. He watched them disappear inside Ike Norton's home.

"Wait here," he ordered the Yaqui, and slipped, a dark shadow in the night, toward the back of the County Commissioner's.

The Masked Rider could stalk as well as any Indian; Blue Hawk had taught him plenty of tricks and he had learned the expert ways of the tracker. From spot to spot of cover the black-clad hombre now flitted, unseen by gunmen eyes blinded by town lights.

Reaching Ike Norton's back yard, he slipped around the dark side to the lighted windows of a front room. Listening, he could hear the murmur of voices in there. He stuck the blade of his strong knife in the crack at the sash bottom, eased it up an inch so he could make out the words of those inside.

Pat Grole was talking. Morgan recognized the big sheriff's harsh tones:

"— I'd shot ev'ry damn one, but there was too many citizens around, Ike. Flynn wants everything to look right for a while. However, they'll be dead inside an hour."

"Be careful, will you?" begged Norton.

"Shore, don't git excited; nobuddy'll blame me. If pris'ners try to escape they hafta be shot down."

"S'pose they refuse to leave jail?"

Grole laughed. "They'll go, 'cause the way'll seem clear. They'll be forced out if need be. I'll have gunnies hid up on the roof corner, and when them lousy cowmen sneak underneath, they'll be shot — escapin'. I knowed that old coot Woods had snaked into town. One of my men spied 'em on their way in, so I hustled here. Vern Flynn had me send a rider acrost the Line to fetch some old pals of his to help. I'm pickin' them up 'cause we got to clean the chaparral quick; we've about won and we'll be rich. It'll be plumb easy to smash them ranchers now we got Woods and the main leaders."

"You saw the Chief in the hills?" Norton asked cautiously.

"Yeah. Flynn's got it all figgered, like he said when he brought us in. He's one smart hombre, the Chief is. Things're workin' perfect, jist like he claimed. I'm shore glad he came our way, Ike. He's wanted for murder up nawth, but when we win here he'll have money enough to buy hisself off. Well, I'll be goin'. Got to snatch a few winks. The hull business'll be settled inside the next hour."

"I hope there's no slip-up," said Norton anxiously. "I — I saw that Masked Rider, Grole. He's a holy terror, I've heard."

Grole cursed furiously. "I'll nail his hide up and collect the rewards on him. He tried to slow me down, but he's lost out."

"He's a tough rascal. Be keerful. Wish we could have got him on our side."

Grole laughed grimly. "I'll shoot him dead next time we meet. From what I've heard he's apt to horn in on the side of people like Woods, savvy? He'd be no use to me the way these other gunnies are."

"What'll you do if they try to horn in on the big money?"

Grole laughed again. "Huh. If they don't keep their side of the bargain, I'll not keep mine. Ain't but a few might kick over the traces; they're glad to have a safe county to live in. They kin raid others, and a few dollars' wuth of likker'll satisfy 'em. Those that kick I'll sell their pelts where they're wanted. Okay, Ike, yuh're doin' fine, Flynn says. Keep it up."

The clink of spurs, slam of a door, told the listener the crooked sheriff was on his way. Crouched at the end of the porch, the Masked Rider glimpsed the dark figure of the officer as Grole hustled across the plaza toward the city hall.

"Flynn — Vern Flynn," he muttered, to print the name on his brain. "He's one of the chief claimants on this range — and he shore must be Grole's boss and the one who planned it all!"

And there was wholesale murder being plotted, the wiping out of Woods and his friends, leaders of the hapless cowmen.

"Gotta stop that," he said, turning to

hurry back to where Blue Hawk held the horses.

The Yaqui took his orders in silence, nodded, swung into the gray's saddle and rode in a wide arc that would bring him to the other side of town.

The Masked Rider checked his guns, circled around to a spot where he could command the rear exits of the town hall. Dismounting, he crouched there, waiting in the shadows outside. His keen eyes sought the parapet. Rewarded for his patience at last, he saw the dark shape of a Stetson bob up at the northeast corner of the fortlike structure. Watching closely, he soon glimpsed another, then a third. There were men, killers silently awaiting their prey, up there on the roof, just as Grole had told Ike Norton there would be.

A long rifle barrel glinted in the dim light. Overhead, the heavens were dotted with myriad stars, and the moon glowed yellow as it slowly arced across the sky.

He did not have long to wait. A bolt clicked at the back door of the town hall, and he saw blurs that were men emerge and turn north along the 'dobe wall. The rifle barrels above stuck through embrasures and swung to pin the escaping cowmen whose unsuspecting hearts beat high with hope of escape.

The two in front, a horizontal shadow between them, walked heavily, feet sinking in the sandy soil. The Masked Rider stared an instant, then nodded.

"Carryin' Woods. Must be still out," he figured. "But he ain't dead."

Thorny Woods was the horizontal shadow, strung between two pals. The others bunched behind, ready to spell their mates in toting their leader, and heading, evidently by direction of supposed helpers who had released them from their cells in the thick-walled fort, toward the chaparral beyond the north corner of the town hall.

Both heavy Colts gripped in his hands, his grim face a masked blob in the night, the Masked Rider turned toward the murderous drygulchers up on the parapet.

The instant had come. He raised his pistols as the nearest of the winchester barrels stopped its movement covering the ranchers who walked so ignorantly into the death trap set by the fiendish Grole.

He pulled the trigger of his righthand revolver, and saw the red flash of the exploding rifle downward, heard the sharp, startled yelp of the gunman at the embrasure. Then both pistols began roaring, spattering a hail of lead against the serrated teeth of the parapet, a deadly fire that rattled the killers up there on the roof, forced them to fall flat behind the protecting wall, their rifles harmlessly going off in the air, or clattering as they dropped from unnerved hands.

The cowmen stopped, the sudden outbreak of gunshots alarming them. It was warning enough. In the open door through which a tool of Grole's had released them, the Masked Rider saw the cursing turnkey drawing a pistol, to attempt the slaughter of the cowmen. He swung his left Colt that way, and a single smashing bark of the gun doubled the man up on the sill.

"This way," shouted the Masked Rider, "this way, ranchers!"

Keeping up the heavy fire that spiked the terrible plot to wipe out Thorny Woods and his pals, he leaped to his saddle and urged the black stallion along the ragged chaparral rim. His accurate lead forced the drygulchers to cower down behind the shelter of the parapet. One showed his Stetson against the sky, rifle aimed to bring down a victim. At the roar of the heavy Colt in Morgan's hand, he fell back with a shriek that cut off short in a death rattle.

The cowmen saw the avenging rider as he swept into view, and a hoarse shout of hope rose in their throats. They fled, and he covered their retreat with his bullets.

Blue Hawk, having carried out his beloved Senor's commands, shoved forth the saddled horses which the ranchers had left at the livery stable corral, rifles still in place in saddle boots. Quickly the hard-pressed cowmen mounted, one riding double and holding Thorny Woods across the saddle. In a minute they trotted into the brush and out of sight.

Shouts gave the alarm, and Grole gunnies came running around to the rear of the city hall. But it was too late. Citizens, hearing the hubbub, joined the rush, and the alleys leading to the back lane were filled with men. A harsh voice sounded above the rest. Pat Grole ran out, buckling on his gun belts, driving his followers after the fleeing prisoners.

The Masked Rider galloped up to the party of Chaparral County ranchers, called, "Follow me!"

He took the lead, and obediently, never questioning the motives of the mysterious, black-clad hombre who stood between them and death, they fell into line. Blue Hawk showed on the gray, covering the rear of the party, a wraith in the darkness.

The enraged Sheriff Grole, bellowing

orders, was shouting for horses to pursue the escaped victims of his plot. His mad bellowing faded into the darkness behind them. The Masked Rider hurriedly escorted the ranchers to the west side of the town, and drawing aside in the chaparral, waved them on toward home.

"Ride!" he cried, "Ride hell-for-leather, gents!"

"Thanks, Rider — thanks a-mighty," called "Rio" Larris, who owned a spread to the west of the Rabbit Leg. The rest echoed his sentiments, and then they swept out of sight, heading for home.

Blue Hawk pounded into sight. "Senor — they come," he reported. "Sheriff and many hombres."

The shaft of silver moonlight fell on the grim figure of the Masked Rider, ominous with the black domino mask, ominous to the evil doers of the land. He turned in his saddle, waiting with fresh-loaded Colts for the van of Grole's pursuit.

It was not long in arriving. The detour around Mescal town had taken several minutes, during which the big officer had quickly rallied his killers, mounted them and started them off westward, guessing that the ranchers would head for home.

The heavy beat of big horses, the gruff

shouts of lieutenants, told the Masked Rider they were coming, and he waited there at the bend, cool, muscles relaxed, ready. In the Yaqui's brown hands rested a Winchester, barrel pointed on the back trail.

The Masked Rider fired a warning shot as the forerunners of Grole's killer-horde rounded into view. They saw the Rider there, pulled their reins hard with shouts of hate in which fear was mingled, for they had experienced the deadliness of those heavy guns.

Wild bullets whirled about the black-clad hombre's Stetson. Blue Hawk's rifle blazed, and a gunny crashed from his horse. The others fell back in confusion to await the coming of their mates. When the crush arrived, urged on by the cursing, infuriated Grole, and swung the bend with lead tearing the air like a solid wall, the Masked Rider turned and galloped away.

Thus he led them on, catching them at the twists and dips in the trail, ambushing the leaders who pressed forward. They came slower and slower, as no one cared to ride the van. Half a dozen had felt the stinging lead of the Masked Rider and the almost unseen ghost on the gray horse, that was Blue Hawk.

CHAPTER X
CRY FOR HELP

Nearly three hours the terrific, run-and-fight battle continued. Raving, foaming with fury, Sheriff Grole could not force his hired gunmen to make a really determined effort against the guns of the Masked Rider, so elusive yet so deadly. None wished to face the certain death that would be his should he ride upon those Colts.

"Reckon they've got a right good start, even carryin' Woods," he told Blue Hawk, as they shoved fresh cartridges into their guns, a few hundred yards from the oncoming, growling mob.

"Si, Senor — but I hear, I hear!"

"What?" demanded Morgan.

Then he, too, caught the sound of shooting to the west.

"Grole's got patrols out; they must've run into one," he muttered, swinging Midnight that way. "We gotta save these men, Blue Hawk; they're the chief ranchers in the section. If they're killed it'll mean the end for the decent folks in Chaparral County!"

The howling horde was gingerly approaching the bend which the Rider and his fighting companion had just left behind.

As the Masked Rider drove full-tilt west, riding like the born centaur that he was, the flashing black legs of the giant stallion skilfully flying over the rough trail, he caught sight of two riders heading toward him, heavy-set hombres with drawn Colts and glinting eyes.

"Hey — here comes the Masked Rider!" bellowed the one in front. His gun whirled up, spat red-yellow flashes, slugs whipping past the bent head of the black-clad hombre.

The Masked Rider's pistol took the gunman out. The second dragged his right rein, hit the wall of bush. Then Blue Hawk's Winchester rapped once, and the second killer went headfirst over his saddle horn into the mesquite.

Two hundred yards farther on the victors heard heavy firing to the south, saw the fresh-broken path through the dense chaparral from the trail.

Blue Hawk got down from the gray, eyes and hands on the trail. Quickly, he reported,

"Senor, they turn off here — others after them."

A quarter mile in, through a way smashed by the bodies of the rancher chief's horses, they came upon a slight rise in the land where a small hill, cut up by rock outcrops, rose in view against the heavens. A circle of Grole's men, the gunnies he had left in the chaparral, had formed about this spot, shooting at the nest of rocks above.

As he quickly scanned the scene, Wayne Morgan took in the strategy of the terrain. There was the black opening that looked like a cave, screened by jagged boulders and thorned brush. Answering flashes of carbines from behind the stone barricades told the Rider that the cowmen were valiantly trying to defend themselves. They had evidently just made the cave, of which they would have knowledge from their familiarity with the neighborhood, before Grole's patrol hit them. Their horses had been shot down. At the foot of the nest, stretched in full view was the dead body of Rio Larris. Bringing up the rear, he had died, giving his life to protect and shield his friends.

Morgan's Colts began raging at the Grole gunmen. They glimpsed him for an instant, hoarse yells rising on the powder-stung, vibrant air.

"The Masked Rider — the Masked Rider! Git him, boys!"

"No time, no time," muttered Morgan.

"The sheriff," Blue Hawk told him.

Yes, Grole was coming with a hundred more men. The gunnies who had treed the cowmen had dismounted and taken to cover, so there was no way to rout them and free their victims in the few minutes remaining. The Masked Rider could hear the hoarse shouts of Pat Grole and his oncoming devils; bullets whipped the chaparral like hail from the south.

"C'mon," he ordered. "It's shore death to stick here, Blue Hawk. We kin do 'em more good by livin'."

He turned Midnight, and the giant black stallion hit the wall of brush, the "pop" drowned in the heavy gunfire. Blue Hawk following, he retreated westward.

Behind them, the dawn threatened the eastern sky.

Bob Harrison sniffed the aromatic air of the chaparral as he slowly rode the trails south and east of the Ruby Hills. A trained engineer, the young man was making a preliminary survey of the land, necessary to the plans of the Chicago Mining Company for the development of the gold mining property on which he had just taken an option.

He was observing the slope of the land and the drainage of the small creeks that meandered through the dense thorned jungles. It was very early, the sun just reddening the eastern sky. He had left his expert, David Rose, at the mine to continue his assay work.

"Wonderful air down here," he murmured, his clear eyes seeking the east.

That way lay the Rabbit Leg ranch, where he had met Louise Woods. He kept thinking about the pretty young woman, wondering if he had impressed her as she had him.

"We'll pay her grandfather a good sum for his range," he thought.

A reservoir from which to pump the large amounts of water used in refining and to supply inhabitants who would work in the mines, would have to be built; railroad tracks must be laid, a spur to join the mainline; and no doubt a mushroom town would spring up, outsiders rushing to the scene to try their luck in the new diggings. Land would soar skyhigh, and the more the Chicago Mining Company owned, the safer it would be. Harrison had many problems to consider.

He laughed at himself as he realized that he had worked his horse farther and farther east. Hearing the shouts of men, he guessed he was close to the Rabbit Leg Ranch. Pushing up a trail he struck, he was challenged by grim-faced, armed waddies, who recognized him as a dude and a previous visitor.

"Could I get a drink of water?" he asked.

"Shore," replied Shorty, who was in charge.

Harrison found the ranch yard crowded with armed cowboys and ranchers. They were hastily cramming bullets into their belts and pockets, grabbing rifles, arming to the teeth, and saddling up horses. At the north gate on a gray horse sat a tall, broad-shouldered waddy Harrison had seen during his previous visit. This man was grimly waiting for the party of fighters, his face bloodied by several bullet wounds. He had obviously been in a scrap not long before.

Harrison found the cool blue eyes of this man regarding him thoughtfully. He nodded, smiled a greeting which the waddy gravely returned. Then he saw Louise Woods, standing with her hands clasped, a look of deep sadness on her lovely face. He dismounted, and, forgetting the others about, strode to her.

Led by Wayne Morgan, the armed cowmen started to the main east-and-west trail.

115

A handful were left behind to defend the ranch.

"Good morning," Harrison said to the young woman.

She turned her eyes to him. They were greatly worried, and she bit her red lip as she nodded to the engineer.

"What's the matter?" he asked her. "Where are your men going? Is there trouble?"

She only shook her head. Frontier folk, he knew, though hospitable enough, were slow to trust strangers.

"Come in," she invited, "and have some breakfast."

"Thank you."

He followed the pretty young woman inside. The keen tang of the air had made him hungry, and Louise sat with him while he drank coffee and ate hot biscuits. But her worry was so deep she could not keep up the polite conversation he started.

Voices sounded in the yard. Looking out the nearby, open window, Harrison saw his mining competitor Albert LaSalle, riding up with the giant Swede, Oley King. LaSalle's face was dour; he was still angry, Harrison knew, at having been beaten to the big strike in the Ruby Hills. LaSalle dismounted, and Harrison heard him say to Oley:

"I'll be right out. Once we get to Mescal, I figure we can beat that fool Harrison."

LaSalle came into the kitchen, started as he saw Harrison sitting there. He scowled without greeting Harrison, turned his back on the young engineer and spoke to the girl.

"I met a rider on the trail, Miss Woods, who says there's trouble between here and town. Do you think I can get through?"

"Yes. I don't believe they'll bother people like you. If you don't stop a stray bullet you'll be all right."

"Thanks. May I have a drink?"

He accepted the dipper she fetched, refused her invitation to eat, thanked her politely and stalked out.

"He's inside, damn his eyes," he growled audibly to the waiting Swede.

Bob smiled, shrugged. He had an airtight option that gave him first chance at the gold mine in the Ruby Hills, and he could afford to smile at LaSalle's actions.

Louise kept looking through the east window, greatly troubled, listening.

At last Harrison said, "I wish you'd tell me about it. Perhaps there's something I can do to help you, Miss Woods."

She stared straight into his eyes for a long moment. Then, evidently deciding through some feminine intuition that she could fully

117

trust this young stranger, she answered in a steady voice but with a repressed emotion that touched him.

"My grandfather and some of his friends are trapped east of here by a horde of killers. That waddy you saw — his name's Morgan — fetched the word, and our boys have gone to try to save them, though it means a terrible battle, for Grole's got many more fighters than we have."

Harrison had come from the sheltered East, but during his mining work he had visited many rough spots and knew that frontier folk had to defend themselves against such attacks.

"I'll go see if I can do anything for your people," he announced, rising.

Alarm flashed across her lovely face, she put a hand on his sleeve to restrain him. "Oh, no! Thanks, but it's our fight. And very dangerous. You — well, you —"

"I'm a dude, I know," he smiled. "But I've got a gun and I can fight. I can't sit here drinking coffee while your grandfather's being murdered. Just what's it all about? Tell me quickly."

In a few words Louise informed him of Sheriff Grole's persecution, of the newly formed county and its land law. Indignation flushed Harrison.

"I know what these fellows are after! There's a rich gold mine in the Ruby Hills which will make this part of the range extremely valuable. They want title to your land so they can sell it to my company or to people who'll rush in here when news of the strike leaks out."

"But is there anything you can do to stop it?"

"Does your grandfather claim the Ruby Hills?"

She shook her head, reluctantly, Harrison thought. "We've all of us used the hills for common range but never registered them. I reckon anybody who has legally filed the hills, owns them. We'd be satisfied with the area around our ranch."

"No doubt Worrell's bunch has already covered their mine. If I refuse to buy the gold mine, then Albert Lasalle, of the Arizona Syndicate — the man who was here just now — will snap it up. He's been one jump behind me all along and is furious at me for beating him to it. Provided our attorney, John Keith, whom I left in Mescal to search land titles in this section, okays the deal, what I *can* do is to take up our option on the hills and then offer you people our assistance in holding on to your range."

Louise shook her head sadly. "I'm afraid

Grole and his killers — the sheriff's picked up a bunch of gunmen, you know, as fighter's — have got in ahead of us. My grandfather's an old-timer; he never registered his title, even in old Webb County, and the new law of Chaparral legally takes away his land."

"Just the same, Keith may find a loophole for you. And right now I'm going to ride and help your friends."

She tried to stop him, but Harrison was determined to go. He mounted, smiled down into her pretty, anxious face, and started east along the trail.

He rode for an hour, the sun rising warmly golden in his eyes. The distant sound of heavy firing grew distinct; evidently a gun battle of large proportions was raging ahead. As he drew nearer, the aromatic air of the chaparral was made hideous by explosions of shotguns, pistols and rifles; yells of the fighting men led Harrison through freshly driven paths to the rock nest where Thorny Woods had been toted by his sore-pressed comrades.

The young engineer sniffed the acrid odor of powder smoke, blown to his nostrils by the breeze. He heard slugs zipping in the leaves, thudding into wood and dirt, ricocheting with eerie shrieks from the rocks.

The Rabbit Leg men, cowboys and ranchers driven to band together by Grole's gunnies and gathered under Wood's head, had come up through the bush. With the aid of Wayne Morgan, they had run the enemy back from the west side of the nest, with its sheltering cavern. Lined up, using trees and stones for cover, the two opposing bands now were shooting it out. By the Rider's help the rancher's were slowly winning, successfully holding off their enemies, though it was a costly fight.

Bravely Harrison kept on. The fire at his left was very strong, for Grole outnumbered the ranchers. Harrison could sense the hot hatred in the atmosphere, the fury of clashing factions and he felt insignificant, helpless. How could one man stop a war?

He shouted, drawing the attention of both sides. Neither bunch troubled to shoot at the dude.

"Stop — let's talk this over," Harrison called. He waved his arms, walking steadily toward the line of fire.

CHAPTER XI
AMAZING ARMISTICE

Leaden death was close to the young engineer. He shouted again, and saw a tall, broad-shouldered man, with wiry black beard stubble on high-boned cheeks and an eagle beak of a nose start toward him, ducking from tree to tree. The sun caught the silver badge on the tall fellow's vest. Harrison rightly concluded this must be Sheriff Pat Grole of whom he had heard.

Grole craned his neck as though he found it hard to believe that he saw Harrison coming. Suddenly he turned and bellowed in a stentorian voice that roared over the gunfire.

"Hold yore fire, boys! Don't hurt that dude, savvy?"

Sheriff Grole took care not to expose his hide to the sharp-shooting ranchers. He crept along till he could speak to Bob.

"Listen, feller, yuh'll git yoreself kilt if yuh hang around these parts. Hustle, ride outa it."

Harrison stubbornly shook his head, stood his ground. Grole turned to curse angrily at a couple of gunnies who were still firing, in spite of their captain's command.

"Hold it, damn yore eyes," he bellowed.

His perturbation at sight of Harrison, his obvious solicitude for the young Easterner's well being, astounded the engineer. The tall sheriff stood erect behind a thick tree trunk.

"What yuh want, Mister? Don't yuh know any better than to horn in here?" he growled.

"Sheriff, stop this, it's murder," Harrison cried angrily, face flushed. "These ranchers are only defending their lives and property."

Grole's fierce, red-tinted eyes glowed. Harrison saw the bulldog jaw, caught the officer's muttered cursing. A tough gunny nearby snickered.

"Lemme take keer of the dude, Grole," he remarked. "I'll show him." And a big Colt rose to pin Bob.

"Drop that gun, yuh crazy fool," Grole snarled quickly. "If yuh shoot this dude, I'll drill yuh myself, savvy?"

He was plainly upset at Harrison's presence and Bob didn't understand why. The sheriff went on, almost pleadingly, to Harrison:

"Please git outa here. I got to do my duty

and arrest these men; they've committed murder and kept me from carryin' out the law."

"If you really believe in legal means," said Harrison coolly, "I'd advise you to stop this slaughter and call off your men. Here's my card: I'm Robert Harrison, of the Chicago Mining Company. I know what you're after. Your friends want this range because of the gold strike in the Ruby Hills."

Grole glowered at him, but made no move to attack. He glanced at the card, shrugged.

"Now look," he growled, "all this is legal, Harrison. Claims've bin filed on this land, and these so-called ranchers're jist squatters resistin' the law. They gotta git out. Will yuh please ride away now so yuh don't git kilt?"

"No, I won't. I'll stay here, Sheriff, and try to see justice done."

"All right," said Grole. "We'll stop."

A stunned silence hung over the field of battle where dead men and horses lay about. Wayne Morgan, watching the strange scene from a pile of rocks in the front of the rancher position, was as astonished as Harrison when Grole stopped the fight at the dude's insistence.

"Hey, Grole," a gunny called insistently, creeping up from the south, "this is a good chanct to rush 'em. They've quit shootin'.

What's the idee of quittin' now?"

"Shut up," Grole snarled.

Wondering eyes peeped from the rock nest and the shelter the ranchers and cowboys had seized. Wayne Morgan had seen Bob Harrison coming up, had tried to shout a warning to the dude to keep back. The fact that Grole would stop the fight for Harrison was so astounding that Morgan and the cowmen could hardly credit what they saw.

And now Harrison coolly stepped right out to the middle of the battlefield and stood there with folded arms. Firing from either side would mean he would be caught, killed.

Grole was livid, teeth gritted. "Git back and find yore hosses," he snapped at his men.

"Like hell," an angry gunman replied. "We got 'em cornered, and we're goin' to take 'em, eh, boys?"

A roar of approval greeted this. But Grole, whipping up his Colt, faced them.

"Damn yuh — yuh'll ruin the hull game if yuh kill that dude," he said, voice low, insistent. "Tell yuh later. C'mon, git back."

The killers hesitated, calmed down some. Then they began to fade back into the bush, to find their mounts and leave the scene. Bob Harrison watched them, a puzzled crease between his clear eyes. In spite of his bold stand, he was astonished at his easy victory. Presently he no longer heard Grole and his retreating killers.

Wayne Morgan had brought help in the nick of time to keep Grole from overwhelming the handful of fugitives in the cave. Now an engineering dude had bluffed off the sheriff. Cowmen were scratching their heads in bewilderment as they stared at the dude who, with a few words, had driven Grole off. It didn't make sense.

"Look out, boys, mebbe it's a trap," growled a gruff voice.

Thorny Woods had come back to life. The scalp crease in his white-haired head was bandaged under his hat. He had regained consciousness during the ride, and had been shooting his old Frontier Model Colt with the best of them during the battle.

Bob Harrison found his horse, and joined the ranchers. He stayed with them as they beat a retreat through the chaparral; and they were neither ambushed nor pursued. Carrying their wounded, the line of fighting men pushed steadily toward the Rabbit Leg Ranch. Bob Harrison found Wayne Morgan close to him.

"How'd yuh manage to send Grole off?" Morgan asked him curiously. "What'd yuh say to him, Harrison?"

Harrison shrugged.

"It surprised me it was so easy, Morgan. I told him it was illegal, and I'd stay here and die rather than let him injure you men. He seemed to be afraid I'd get hurt. I heard Grole say it would ruin the game if I was killed — though what he meant I can't tell you."

"The game — wonder what kinda game," murmured the waddy.

There was, Morgan thought, just one game Sheriff Grole must be thinking of, and that was the gold mine in the Ruby Hills. The sheriff was connected with it, and Grole's extreme solicitude for Bob Harrison's hide was the most telling clue which the Rider had yet come upon. If they had gold in the Hills, then it was good for anybody, and not just for the Chicago Mining Company.

They hit the Rabbit Leg at noon, straggling in. Louise ran out to throw her arms around Thorny Woods; the old fellow grinned as she kissed his weather-beaten cheek.

"Oh, Granddad," she cried. "You — you're not hurt badly, are you? I'm so glad you beat those brutes off."

Woods stalking to the house, an arm

around Louise, jerked a thumb at Harrison.

"Thank that young man, baby. Alone and single-handed he told Grole to stop fightin' and dang my wuthless hide if the sheriff didn't hang his head and slink off. Never seen sich a thing in my life. Jest the same," he added seriously, "we're obleeged, Bob, and anything we got is yores."

Harrison felt richly rewarded for his trouble when Louise smiled on him. He had climbed higher in her estimation. When she had made her grandfather comfortable inside, she came to join Harrison.

"I don't know how to thank you," she said. "It was mighty good of you."

Harrison took her hand. "I'm glad I could do it. And tomorrow I'm going to Mescal and see what I can do about your land." At the warmth of her hand a thrill went through his heart. Her eyes were kind and he knew he loved this sweet, courageous girl.

"I'll be back," he promised her. "Everything's going to work out well for you. My company will take over the Ruby Hills, provided my assayer gives a good final report, and then I'll be able to help you."

Again she thanked him, shyly. He was shaken by the new emotion which had seized him.

"I'll have to leave you," she told him. "I

must care for the wounded."

He released her hand, turned when she went inside with a final wave and smile to him. Harrison prepared in a daze to leave. As he was mounting, Wayne Morgan strolled over.

"Yuh reckon yuh'll buy that gold mine, Harrison?" he inquired.

"Yes, if the land titles are clear and my assayer gives the lode a good report."

"Take my advice, and make a careful check. Grole's hooked up to that mine somehow, and the way he acted today with yuh when he stopped that fight on your lone say-so, cinches the fact that they're handlin' yuh with kid gloves for some reason of their own."

"What could that reason be? If the gold's there, we can't lose, and Rose will know."

Morgan nodded. "Yeah, that's true, if the gold's there," he said enigmatically, and drew away as Harrison left in a hurry to get back to the Hills.

It was near supper time when Bob Harrison reached the gold camp. The miners were not working, were lounging around. Lobster Jake greeted the engineer.

"Where yuh bin?" Worrell asked. "I sent a couple of the boys to hunt yuh. Figgered yuh mighta run into the bandit who held up LaSalle."

"No, Jake." Harrison told the squat, red-faced boss about his eventful day. "Is it true?" he demanded sternly, "that Grole's hooked up with you, Worrell?"

"No, it ain't," snapped Jake. "On'y as sheriff of the county, that's all. And, say, we got a watertight title here, Harrison, yuh needn't worry 'bout that. Look it up in the land records in Mescal. As for the range, that ain't my bus'ness. Reckon somebuddy found out about this gold strike and is tryin' to grab it 'fore rushers come in."

Harrison nodded. He was worn out, wanted to eat, and rest for his trip to Mescal. "Where's Dave Rose?" he inquired. "Has he finished his assay?"

"Yeah. He fell off'n a ladder and skinned his face some. But he ain't hurt bad. He's in yore tent."

Lobster Jake went over with the engineer. David Rose was stretched on a cot, an arm flung across his eyes. There was a rough bandage, stained with blood, on his right cheek.

"Hello, Dave — are you hurt much?" asked Harrison quickly.

Rose's voice was weak as he replied, "No, no, I'm all right."

"Have you finished your survey?"

"Yes, pretty much." Rose cleared his throat.

"And —" prompted Harrison.

"It's the richest mine I've ever seen, Bob."

"What'd I tell yuh?" crowed Lobster Jake, from the door flap.

Darkness fell on the Ruby Hills. Bob Harrison retired early. In the dawn he would ride for Mescal, connect with Lawyer John Keith, telegraph his report and receive by return wire authority to purchase the fabulously rich gold mine.

Funds were kept by the Chicago Company in a Houston, Texas, bank. Keith and Harrison could give checks and notes in the transaction which could be cashed in Houston. Mescal had a bank, but it was too small to handle more than a part of the large turnover in cash.

"Just the same," Harrison thought, "I'll take no chances down here. Keith can figure how to handle the deal."

CHAPTER XII
ONE-SHOT JACKSON

Wayne Morgan, worn down by the terrific fighting job of snatching Thorny Woods and the rancher chiefs from the jaws of death, ate a hearty meal at the Rabbit Leg Ranch. Louise and the other women pressed food and drink on him, and could not show enough gratitude to this wandering waddy who had helped their men.

He was exceeded in their esteem only by the mysterious Masked Rider who had several times flashed up at crucial moments to stand with his accurate guns between them and their enemies. There was much speculation as to who the Masked Rider really was.

The yard was crowded, as were the buildings, with women and children, fathers of families, cowboys and old fellows, all fugitives from the surrounding range who had gathered at the Rabbit Leg. There was talk about Bob Harrison who had, with a few words, sent Sheriff Pat Grole slinking off. That, all agreed, was about as close to a miracle as they would ever see. That a strange young dude, without so much as drawing a gun, could shoo away a fighter of Grole's reputation and a hundred gunmen, was simply unbelievable.

Embarrassed by the thanks heaped on him, Morgan slipped across the yard to the hay loft to indulge in needed sleep. Guards were out around the ranch, and the afternoon hours quickly passed; dark fell, and the broad-shouldered hombre, resting in the soft hay, napped on, renewing his vitality.

He slept through the darkness; there was no alarm or trouble to rouse him. The cowmen, too, were grateful for a chance to rest. A forage party which rode out to bring in beef for food came back with their steers, reporting they had not been attacked and had seen no sign of the enemy.

The sun was rising in a clear sky when Wayne Morgan finally woke up. Going down the ladder, he stepped into the yard and went to the pump to wash up. Tantalizing odors of coffee and frying food reached him on the light breeze rustling the waving chaparral.

Alert, his brain was busy formulating questions as he thought back over the events of the past days. The question that bothered him most was, why had Sheriff Grole backed down for the young dude, Bob Harrison? On account of the sale of the big gold mine to Harrison's company?

Morgan knew there was a connection between Lobster Jake Worrell and Pat Grole. The sale depended largely on Harrison's okay. Legally title to the hills and to the surrounding land would be cleared in Mescal by Norton, by use of the new land law passed depriving these ranchers of their homesteads.

"Why?" he wondered aloud, as he rubbed his face pink on the rough towel by the pump. "Why should Worrell and Grole worry 'bout what Harrison thinks, if they've got such a good mine up there? They could sell it to any mining development company — LaSalle's Arizona Syndicate or another."

He shook his head, started over to ask some breakfast from Louise Woods.

Bob Harrison appeared, riding in from the east-and-west trail. He stayed but a few minutes, speaking with Louise. Morgan observed the liking the two were developing for one another.

"They're nice lookin' young folks," he thought, watching them say goodby.

Harrison told the girl he was on his way

to Mescal, and that he would there do everything possible to advance the cowmen's interests. Morgan shook his head as the stalwart young engineer passed the ranch guards and disappeared in the brush on his way to town.

"Still don't savvy Grole's play," he muttered. "And where's this Flynn, the chief of 'em all, come in? Like to catch that hombre."

In the afternoon, Morgan heard the distant, eerie call of Blue Hawk. It was easy for him, trusted as he was here, to slip away on the gray horse and connect with his Yaqui friend who was waiting in the bush for him off the main trail to Mescal.

"What yuh got, Blue Hawk?" he inquired, greeting the Indian.

"Senor, I watch the sheriff as you order."

"Yeah — and what?"

Blue Hawk reported. He had, a wraith in the dense bush, kept an eye on Grole as Morgan had told him to. Bob Harrison had passed on his way to Mescal. An hour later along had come the red-faced Lobster Jake Worrell, with a number of armed, tough miners. Worrell drove, announced Blue Hawk, a pack horse with two large wooden boxes strapped on its back. They had turned south off the east-west path and joined up with Grole. Now Grole and Lobster Jake were emptying a couple of bottles of whiskey together, talking things over.

"What yuh s'pose they brought in those boxes," Morgan growled aloud.

The Yaqui shrugged, his black eyes expressionless. "They are very careful, Senor. I see fire marks on boxes."

"Red marks — that means danger." Morgan thought for a moment. "Miners! They'd have blastin' powder and dynamite! That must be it. C'mon, Blue Hawk, we gotta find out what they're plannin'."

The Yaqui scouted the road, with its twistings and turns. He knew the spot where Grole and his killers were camped to the south, hidden in the chaparral, and they made a wide detour to the north on side trails to avoid the sentinels Blue Hawk said were posted there.

With the idea of getting to the east of the sheriff's bunch and so working back from a direction the gunnies would not be expecting trouble to show, they crossed the east-west way a mile beyond the side path to Grole's camp.

Near the road to Mescal they heard the approach of a rider. From a bush screen, dismounted, the two spied the oncoming man. He was a big fellow, with a gray Stetson, grim face smeared with dirt; he wore brown chaps, gloves, and a thick leather jacket that protected against thorns. Plainly a gunman, whose suspicious eyes darted from one side of the path to the other, whose dirty hand was hovering near the butt of his worn Colt.

"Goin' to join Grole," mused Morgan.

He reached back, took the short lariat from Midnight's saddle horn, shook it out. The slight swish of the rope attracted the attention of the gunman; his red horse sniffed loudly and danced as he came along the trail.

"Who's that?" he snarled, paw flashing to his pistol.

The lariat snaked out, rawhide noose settling over the man's shoulders. Morgan yanked it tight, trapping the dropping arms at his sides. Cursing, squirming, the gunman managed to get a Colt out, hammer spur back under his calloused thumb. He gripped the saddle with steel knees, but the Yaqui and Morgan sprang out on him.

With a desperate twist, as he felt himself falling, the hombre swung his pistol on the roper. Blue Hawk leaped high, long knife flashing in the sunlight, but Wayne Morgan's quick jerk sent the gunman's own weapon turning in, his thumb slipped off the ham-

137

mer, the big .45 exploding with a muffled roar against the leather jacket.

He went limp, crashed in the trail. Blue Hawk grabbed the sorrel's bridle, quieting the mustang with a word and a touch of his brown hand.

They dragged the dead man back into the brush. Hunting through his pockets, Morgan found a short note:

Grole: This is One-Shot Jackson from Matamoras. Trust him. For heaven's sake, finish it up, will you? I can't stand it much longer. Claims are already being made, the word's out. Norton.

Wayne Morgan studied the note from the county commissioner to the thieving sheriff. Then he bent over the dead One-Shot Jackson, evidently a known gunman, and began to strip off leather jacket, the Stetson and gloves. Blue Hawk watched his friend with inscrutable eyes as Morgan quickly donned Jackson's outfit, smeared his face with dirt and berry juice until he was scarcely recognizable, and mounted the sorrel mustang.

"You go there, Senor?"

"Yes. I'm goin' to deliver this letter to Grole tonight, soon as it's dark."

The Yaqui said nothing more. He took

138

charge of the gray and Midnight, and they worked back toward the spot where Grole's gang waited in the bush.

When the sun dropped, the Masked Rider, fixed up as One-Shot Jackson, mounted the sorrel, took the main trail and rode boldly toward the sheriff's hideout.

Cookfires were burning in a small clearing, the glows hidden by an overhanging rock wall. The great number of fighting outlaws enlisted by the sheriff lounged around, drinking, eating, playing cards or talking. Guards on the trail challenged the approaching rider. He grunted his name, chin on his breast, and handed over the note from Ike Norton of Mescal.

It was delivered immediately to Sheriff Grole, who came over from the spot where he had been sitting with Lobster Jake Worrell. The disguised Morgan saw two square wooden boxes set on a flat rock. He took in the red stripes, the "DANGER" printed in crimson letters on the explosives, and knew he had guessed right.

Dismounting, he slouched there, the brim of One-Shot Jackson's hat pulled low over his dirt-smeared face. Grole held the note to the firelight, read it quickly, stuck it in his pocket. He hardly glanced at the newcomer.

"Okay, make yourself at home, Jackson," he said. "There'll be work for yuh, pronto."

He turned, strolled back to Lobster Jake, to finish up a bottle they had opened.

Morgan looked over the cruel faces of the hired killers. He mingled with them, but kept his own features in shadow. He accepted some food and drink shoved toward him, and watched Grole and Worrell as they drank, working in as close as he dared.

"Vern Flynn oughta be here soon," he heard Pat Grole remark. "This is all his idee, Jake. It was workin' mighty well till that damn Masked Rider horned in."

"Yeah, and he better figger how to finish this up quick," growled Lobster Jake. "If he holds off much longer there won't be no way to win."

"He will. Flynn's the smartest devil I ever knowed," declared Grole, admiration in his voice.

Flynn! At last Morgan was to see in the flesh the powerful criminal chief to whom Grole gave allegiance, the man who evidently had planned these awful events, had set murder and robbery raging by his evil brain. Flynn, director of the brutal plot against the ranchers of Chapparal.

A half hour later there was a stir to the north, and a strange whistle, a descending, triple-noted shrilling, came from above. Sheriff Grole jumped to his feet, Lobster Jake following more slowly as he shoved up his squat, wide figure.

"There's Flynn," Morgan heard the sheriff say.

The pair of them walked to the path. Morgan, looking about, found no one was observing him. Many gunmen slept, others were too preoccupied to notice him as he edged closer to the spot where the two boxes were set, some yards away from the main bunch. Grole had his kit there, a case of whiskey, and food.

A rider appeared, escorted by Grole and Worrell. Morgan lay flat in the shadow, feigning sleep, his body all but hidden in the high chino grass. He stared keenly at the newcomer.

The man on the fast chestnut horse wore a Mexican's peaked sombrero, pulled low over his eyes. He had on a velvet Spanish cloak, and kept his bandanna pulled up to his nose. If this was Vernon Flynn, Morgan thought, he was certainly keeping himself hidden from all but Grole and Lobster Jake, his lieutenants who worked with him. The rank and file did not know him.

The disguised Chief dismounted and, Grole at one flank and Lobster Jake on the

141

other, strode over to the spot where the sheriff's gear lay. A fresh bottle of whiskey was opened, but the Chief impatiently waved it away.

Morgan could make out the glow of the feline eyes, over the tight-drawn bandanna. Ears wide, holding his breathing back lest he might miss what the three said, he lay pressed to the ground.

"So you missed them again!" Flynn said coldly. "I've told you both exactly what to do — and you muffed it."

His voice was muffled by the mask over his lips. But Morgan had heard that cold, thin snarl before. He had caught its overtones when he had chanced upon the conference in the gulch up near the gold mine, and now he recognized it.

"Well, what could I do," asked Grole defensively. "Hell, Flynn, I hadda pull my men off, onct the dude come along. He mighta got kilt in the shootin', for one thing. For another, I didn't dare rile him any more. He was all roused up, so I figgered I'd best let him have his way. Fust thing yuh know he'd of refused to buy."

"He's gone to Mescal this mornin'," Lobster Jake growled. "I took keer of ev'rything at my end, Flynn."

"Did you bring that dynamite as I sent

you word?"

"Shore, it's right here, Chief." Worrell jerked a stubby thumb toward the two red-marked boxes. " 'Nough there to blow up the hull county."

"I'll have it set myself," Flynn announced. "Grole, your men can be hidden to clean 'em up after we've blown the center to hell."

"Okay," the sheriff agreed. "I on'y hope that Masked Rider's in the middle. Damn his hide. He snatched them cowmen from me at Mescal and he's damn near spoilt our game. Why, I'd of had these squatters plumb outa here before Harrison come along if it hadn't bin for him."

"That was the way I counted on," Vernon Flynn said, "but you managed to fumble it, Grole. I had the whole thing figured out perfectly. Have you any idea where this outlaw rider is now?"

"I s'pose he's hangin' around the Rabbit Leg."

"Huh. Harrison'll spend the next day or two in Mescal, anyway. That gives us a chance to clean up. Understand? When Harrison comes back into this district, I want everything to be quiet and the ranchers already out of the picture."

Grole replied respectfully. "Yes, sir."

"He'll raise hell, Boss, when he finds that

Woods gal gone," declared Lobster Jake, but he, too, gave Vernon Flynn deep respect. "He told me 'bout her, and from what he said, I b'lieve he's in love with her."

"Good. I'll remember that." Flynn's voice was as cold as ice. He gave the impression that a slimy reptile might. His power over Grole and Worrell was obvious, and Morgan had no doubt that he was the master mind of the criminal combination, had planned the awful scheme which had brought murder and desolation to the range.

"Now load those boxes for me," the brutal Flynn went on, "and I'll get goin'. Give me a dozen trusted men and have me covered on the trails."

Vernon Flynn rose, movements decisive. Though on an evil trail he knew just where he wanted to go. Protected by his *vaquero* disguise, yet his strength and arrogance were obvious as he strolled off.

Sheriff Grole obsequiously escorted his master to his mount, then came back, walking toward the spot where Morgan was lying. Suddenly the fierce, tall officer stopped as he saw the long figure of the man supine in the coarse Chino grass. Wayne Morgan kept his eyes veiled by his lids, but watched the sheriff through his lashes. He remained quiet, breathing evenly as though sound asleep. Grole muttered a curse and started on. But suspicion gnawed at him, and he came back and stood over Morgan.

"Hey, you," he growled, stirring the supposed One-Shot Jackson with his toe.

Morgan feigned to arouse. He sat up, blinked, and looked into the hard, bearded face of the giant sheriff.

"What's wrong?" he demanded. "Ready to give me that job I'm to do?"

Grole kept staring at him.

"What yuh doin', lyin' there, feller?" he demanded angrily. "Didn't I tell yuh to stay with the boys?"

"Sorry," muttered Morgan, glancing around. "Ain't I with 'em? Was jist snoozin', Boss —"

"Yuh was listenin' to what the Chief said," accused Grole. He was inflamed, not only by the redhot whiskey he had consumed but by the reprimand of Vernon Flynn. Not yet did he guess that the man at his feet was not the gunman he claimed to be, but he wished to give this snoopy newcomer a lesson in obedience. Grole had to be tough to keep the upper hand over the outlaw crew he had taken on.

He kicked out at Morgan's face, to rake his cheek with the spur. Instinctively Morgan ducked, and the sharp rowel caught in his Stetson strap, taut below his left ear. As the heavy sheriff pulled his leg back, the leather cord snapped, and Morgan's shielding hat flew from his head. His face, turned full to the light of a campfire, showed in the shaft of red illumination.

"Why, damn yuh —" gasped Grole.

Wayne Morgan saw the light of recognition dawn in the fierce eyes of the murderous officer. Grole had had a good look at the supposed wandering waddy who had aided the ranchers and brought help for them. With the hat off, in such light, the sheriff knew who this man was.

CHAPTER XIII
EXIT SHERIFF GROLE

Grole was lightning on the draw, and Morgan was off balance, in an awkward, squatting position. The sheriff stepped back, and his right-hand Colt flashed from its supple holster. The hammer spur was under the calloused, long thumb, and the weapon cocked by its own weight as it cleared leather, muzzle rising to aim at Morgan's brain, the entire draw completed in a sweeping hand flick that consumed only a second-fraction of time.

Wayne Morgan had no time to get out his own weapon. There was no chance to beat the sheriff to the draw, so he tried other tactics. He was moving even as Grole started back in that gunman's movement. Feet dug into the roots of the coarse chino grass, Morgan straightened his powerful legs, shot forward like a rising jack-in-the-box impelled by strong springs.

Grole's pistol roared, the explosion nearly

147

bursting Morgan's ear-drum, which rang maddeningly, deafeningly. He felt the clipping sear that shot tremors of agony through his nerve-ends as the big lead slug ripped through his tousled, dark hair. And then his head butted Grole's chest, sent the sheriff reeling back from the impact of Morgan's lithe, two hundred pound frame.

This play brought Morgan up erect, while Sheriff Grole's rangy figure was staggering back against the firelight. The raging lawman recovered himself. His gun, knocked aside and down, whirled back to position. It flashed a second shot. But just a shade ahead, the unmasked Morgan's heavy Colt, appearing in his hand with a speed which shamed the sheriff's draw, spat red-yellow flame.

The sheriff's second bullet zipped between Morgan's widespread legs, kissing one wing of the leather chaps and burying itself in the dirt. The exposed rider's bullet caught Grole in the breast, and the impact staggered the tall, fierce killer backward. He teetered for a moment, mouth dropping open, eyes going blank.

As Grole half-twisted in his tracks, folding up in the chino grass, the band of killers roused up in bewilderment. Then yells of fury rang out, and men sprang to their feet, digging for their weapons.

Morgan turned even as Pat Grole's heavy body thudded to earth. His two guns in hand, he swung to rake the camp. Up at the north end he saw Lobster Jake and the supposed Mexican who was Vernon Flynn running back at sound of the shots.

Morgan knew he had but a moment in which to escape. A score of guns were turning on him, thirsting to kill the man who had slain Pat Grole.

He moved with the agility of a wild thing. Commanding his trained muscles, he dived headfirst into the wall of chaparral nearby. His body was torn at by the cruel thorns of the brush, but he was gone before a shot was fired. The instant he was out of sight he turned north, at a sharp angle, and then a heavy fusillade of bullets came through the chaparral, passing within a foot of him, some too high, others to the side, but all uncomfortably close.

Sharp rocks, in the dense blackness of the brush, cut his outstretched hands. He eeled around back of them, lay for an instant to orient his eyes while the blindly fired bullets rattled in the stones, perforating the chaparral. He chose not to shoot back, thereby exposing his exact position.

"Torches — git torches!" shouted Lobster

Jake, running across the clearing with the waddling stride of a grizzly bear.

Vernon Flynn, in his Mexican clothes, grabbed up a Winchester rifle, knelt and began systematically combing the bush, at belly height of a man, with the accurate, cool fire of an expert. The concentrated fire forced Morgan to lie quiet, until the gunnies snatched up burning brands to light the way and started after him.

The brutal Flynn now took charge of the chase. He was much cleverer, more devilishly destructive than Grole or Worrell. Under his directions, they began cutting through the brush. Morgan had to move, and he crawled away, keeping low, moving parallel with the uneven edge of the clearing.

In a brief lull, above the shouting of the killers, Morgan heard Blue Hawk's inquiring call. When he answered it, he pressed down flat, for that drew the rifle shots from Flynn again his way.

"There he is — after him, kill him!" the chief roared.

Morgan was still afoot. Blue Hawk was some distance to the north, but coming in, for he had heard the first shots and immediately guessed his friend was in trouble.

Morgan, face bleeding from the swipe of

brutal thorns, wormed his way through the chaparral. A hundred yards above the clearing, he came on a twisting, narrow cow trail through the bush. Gratefully he followed it, making better time. Flynn was cleverly guessing his position, however. The bush seemed alive, behind him, with his pursuers, shouting, shooting wildly, waving their red torches as they came on.

Panting for breath, wounds bleeding profusely, Morgan limped on. Blue Hawk called again, closer. He answered, and once more the bullets whined too near for comfort.

The long line of gunmen, spread out through the bush, cut him off from retreat westward. He was forced on east as the wings closed in, trying to nip him as they swung. Then he saw the wraithlike figure of his Yaqui friend, leading the two horses along the little cow trail.

"Here I am, Blue Hawk," he sang out, so the Indian would know it was he approaching.

"Senor!" exclaimed the Indian in relief. "Quick!"

Mounted, the two sped east, away from the murderous guns, leaving the noise of the chase behind them.

A mile off, they stopped at a spring Blue

Hawk discovered, a waterhole used by wild brush cattle. Here the skillful Indian washed and bound Morgan's wounds. They let the horses drink sparingly, and Morgan recovered his torn, stained clothing, tossed away what had belonged to One-Shot Jackson, and resumed his Masked Rider garb, settling the black domino mask across his glowing, grim eyes.

"Grole's done for," he told Blue Hawk. "But there's Lobster Jake and that Flynn hombre, who's the big chief of it all. They're plannin' some kind of wholesale killin' with dynamite Worrell brought down, and we got to check 'em."

Heading south, they found another narrow cow track winding back westward toward the Rabbit Leg. But they had made only a short distance when the Masked Rider realized the way was guarded. They almost ran onto a patrol of gunmen. Bullets flew between them, and shouts told Morgan that reinforcements were close at hand.

"We'll try another," he muttered, turning Midnight and striking back for the south path.

But a second time they ran into armed men, hidden, waiting for them on the lower trail.

Scouting several ways west, they found all

152

the routes to the ranch plugged.

"That's Vernon Flynn," reflected the Masked Rider. "He's a right smart sidewinder, Blue Hawk. Hafta figger how to bust through. We can't ride that distance through the chaparral without a trail. Never git there."

"Shoot through, Senor," suggested Blue Hawk.

Morgan nodded. "Yeah, I reckon that's the on'y way."

Guns loaded and ready, they struck a trail three miles south of the gunmen's camp. Advancing stealthily, they ran into a patrol, and this time both the Rider and the Yaqui cut the brush ahead with their accurate fire. A screech of anguish told them they had made a hit in their first calculated volley. They emptied their weapons, driving the sentries back into the chaparral.

On his pet black, the Masked Rider led the way, reloading on the run. Low over Midnight's arched neck, he sped like the wind past the guarded turn, Blue Hawk on the gray at the giant black stallion's flying heels.

Hoarse shouts of fury rang out in the moonlit night; the black shadows of the bush loomed before them as they rode hell-for-leather along the winding trail westward.

Pursuit was taken up, thundering mustang hoofs shaking the earth. The gunmen stuck grimly on their trail for more than a mile, running them, never giving them a chance to rest.

Their faster horses gradually shook off the killers, however. South of the Rabbit Leg, Morgan turned up toward the ranch, but ran into a large bunch of armed riders who were coming from the north. He swung back, cut west on a parallel trail, but again found that the patrols of Vernon Flynn's fighters, thick in the narrow way so they could not smash through, intervened between the ranch and them.

The Masked Rider and his faithful follower, Blue Hawk, backtracked in the moonlit night, hunting for other paths that might take them to the Rabbit Leg, but were blocked in every direction. North, south, east, and west, bandits met them as they approached the stronghold of the Chaparral County cowmen. Hours after his escape from the dead Grole's mob, Morgan had to admit he could not break through the tight, close circle which had been drawn around the ranch. There were no holes, and the bush seemed alive with alert guards.

"Vernon Flynn's taken charge himself, Blue Hawk," growled the black-clad hombre, as they sat their thorn-scratched lathered mounts a half mile south of the ranch clearing, having completed the circle and found no hole. "He's a lot smarter than the others."

He was worried about the dynamite. Flynn, hidden behind his Mexican disguise, was no doubt busy planting it, perhaps within the confines of the Rabbit Leg itself.

Blue Hawk grunted, as he sat his long-legged gray horse. The sky was clear, dotted with a million stars, the moon nearly overhead, silvering the top of the dense chaparral, the shadows inky. Mysterious rustlings, animals shifting in the thorny growth, wild cows stealthily moving to water and feed, crackled the bush.

"Hear that?" the Rider asked suddenly.

Blue Hawk nodded, high-boned, dark face turned toward the west, toward the ranch. A metallic, clinking sound was repeated.

"Shovel on a stone," muttered Morgan. "C'mon. Mebbe we'll find that dynamite yet, Blue Hawk!"

They left their two horses hidden in the thickets, and started worming on foot toward the spot from whence the noise had come. They heard other sounds as they drew in, hunting a path through the dense undergrowth. Soon they saw a reddish light glow ahead. The dark figures of straining men stood out against the ruby illumination.

A couple of dozen gunnies had exchanged their rifles for spades and were running shallow trenches in the earth of the little clearing south of the Rabbit Leg, the same clearing in which the Masked Rider had saved Thorny Woods and his forage party from annihilation when they rode out to hunt beef.

The Masked Rider and the Yaqui lay flat on their bellies, peeking through a tangle of brush at the strange scene.

"That's it," whispered Morgan. "There's the dynamite, Blue Hawk!"

The trenches were about done, and already men were connecting the blasting sticks of explosive with caps and fuses. For an hour the two watched the covering of the murderous stuff, the laying of the terrible death trap. This was Flynn's devilish work, Morgan knew.

"Wonder how they'll draw 'em here?" he mused.

He glimpsed the peaked hat of the masked Mexican he knew as Flynn, as the task of laying the dynamite was finished, and the sod which had been cut off was replaced so nothing would look wrong to men riding over the mined area. Vernon Flynn inspected the job, and the master fuse, covered by dry, coarse chino grass, was laid to a dense thicket at the west of the clearing.

Then three gunmen, selected by the arch-criminal in the peaked sombrero, were picked to guard the hidden end of the fuse. They crawled into the thicket, and the torches were put out. All horses, tools, and signs that anyone had been here, were removed, leaving the clearing empty in the night.

"Gotta control that fuse," breathed the Masked Rider. "Let's go."

Then began a slow stalk, an Indian stalk that occupied nearly two hours of inching along the warm earth, lying still for minutes whenever one of them made an unavoidable sound. They drew closer and closer to the killers who guarded that fuse end. Now and then, a wild steer would raise commotion enough to cover the slight noises they were forced to make in getting through or around great masses of growth.

At last they were so near they could overhear the low, whispered tones of the guards.

"Flynn said not to smoke, but I don't see no hurt in it, do you, boys?" said one.

"Naw, ain't none of them cowmen out this

time of night," replied a second gruffly. "I'm gonna have a quirly."

A match, cupped in a hairy paw, was struck and in its quick flicker the watching, stalking pair saw the cruel faces of the trio.

"Keerful yuh don't tech that there fuse," warned the third.

The three tiny glows of the cigarettes were clearly visible to the Masked Rider and his Indian companion. Separating now, foot by foot, then only inch by inch, the two crept in, the Indian from the west and the Masked Rider from the east.

Never imagining a foe could get to them without betraying himself, the trio of tough gunmen, sprawled on the earth, gun belts slack, talking together in low whispers.

"Reckon that Masked Rider's 'bout beaten," Morgan heard one remark, with a chuckle. "Flynn's too danged smart for him. He got Grole, but Flynn savvies a lot more 'bout this kinda fightin'."

"Yuh're right," agreed a second, a raw-boned, dirty-faced devil with huge hands. "Flynn's jist hidin' behind that mask and clothes —"

The hombre broke off with a gasp of fright, for the Masked Rider suddenly rose up before them, two guns in their faces.

"The first man who moves," Morgan

158

whispered tersely, "dies."

Two shoved their hands quickly overhead. The third, the man with the big paws, spat a curse, growled, "The Masked Rider!" and letting his cigarette drop, clawed for his holstered gun.

From behind him, a white streak shot through the air. There was a scintillating gleam as Blue Hawk's long knife flashed home between the killer's shoulder blades, and the fellow sank back with a muffled groan, collapsing like a pricked balloon.

"Hell's fire!" choked one of the remaining pair. "Now it's Injuns."

The other squeaked with panic as the lithe Indian pulled out the knife, the weapon making a horrid, sucking noise as it emerged, blood spurting in its wake.

Chapter XIV
Swift Justice

Carefully and efficiently the Masked Rider bound and gagged the two fuse guards and rolled them off into the bush.

"Stick here and watch," Morgan ordered Blue Hawk. "I'll fetch yore gray closer. Wait'll I give the signal."

He reckoned on making use of the murderous trap Vernon Flynn had laid.

To the east the sky was lightening, dawn coming up over the tangled jungle of the Nueces. The Masked Rider brought Blue Hawk's gray to a hiding place where the Yaqui could reach the animal hurriedly if necessary. Then, mounting Midnight, he started north toward the Rabbit Leg.

But he knew the path was guarded. Patrols of Flynn's fighters were everywhere. As he paused, watching, he heard a sudden uproar start to the north, at the Rabbit Leg. Men were yelling, guns began banging. Women were screaming confusedly. A fusillade of rifle shots rang out, and defiant yells rose on the damp air of gray dawn.

A full-sized battle was opening as the roar of the guns increased. The Masked Rider waited there in the trail, a deep corrugation showing in his forehead above the domino mask. It was not long until the thud of hoofs coming toward him caused Midnight's ears to prick up. The black stallion snorted, swinging at his master's touch.

Gunmen appeared, the van of a big gang, mounted and fully armed, running ahead of infuriated cowmen urged on by Jim Thorny Woods. The old brush-popper had regained much of his power and was evidently highly incensed, as were his friends and followers. With an insane fury they drove the killers before them. The horde of murderers made little attempt to stand; they were drawing the cowmen on, to the trap south in the chaparral.

The Masked Rider's Colts opened up, and the bandit who had just sighted him left his saddle and hit the dirt with a slug in the chest before he could yell.

"The Masked Rider," screeched a second who saw the black-clad figure with grim, masked face, as Midnight galloped south on the trail.

There were about a hundred hired killers

161

in the bunch which eagerly took up the pursuit, hoping to get their arch-enemy who rode ahead with the mastery of a great horseman. Lieutenants bellowed orders to their men, but Wayne Morgan had not seen the Mexican figure he knew to be Flynn. A few minutes of whirling riding, and he came to the little clearing under which the murderous dynamite was set. He glanced to the west, glimpsed Blue Hawk as the Yaqui stuck up a brown hand to show he was still there and ready.

Close on the Masked Rider's heels came the gunnies, whooping and shooting, their bullets clipping the brush. The killers counted on leading the cowmen to the explosives. Then the hidden mine would be set off, maiming and crippling the ranchers.

The Masked Rider's mountain lion call snarled startlingly loud above the following din. As the gunmen emerged into the clearing, drawing the cowmen to the death trap, a train of sparks spat swiftly through the chaparral, close to the ground.

An instant later, perfectly timed, the mine exploded, catching half the gunnies over the spot. A shattering, ear-splitting crash, that sent rocks, dirt and bush high into the air, enveloping the scene in a great cloud of dust and smoke. It blew men and horses with it,

and the screams of broken creatures pen-
etrated above the echoing noise.

The cowmen, Thorny Woods in the van,
pulled up aghast at the edge of the clearing,
now a crater in the red clay surrounded by
pieces of men and animals. Staring at the
awful sight, the ranchers realized how close
they had come to destruction without
understanding how they had escaped it.

The gunmen who had escaped the blast
had separated into small groups, all fight
gone from their hearts. They were scattering
through the chaparral. Thorny Woods'
stentorian voice now bellowed orders.
Cowboys followed, shooting, giving the
Rebel yell, driving the smashed horde to
surrender or die.

Woods glimpsed the tall rider on the black
stallion, yanked off his Stetson, whirling it
round his bandaged head.

"Hey, Rider — you done that for us, I bet!
Thanks, Mister — thanks."

Midnight flashed on through the winding,
narrow trails, cutting off small bunches of
panic-stricken killers, allowing the ranchers
to take them prisoner or fight it out to the
end.

Old Jim Woods, panting, his Frontier
Model Colt .45 hot in his hand, came riding
back, as the great battle of the chaparral

came finally to its end. Grole's bunch was done for, routed, and the bush was safe for the moment.

The Masked Rider shoved out on the trail in the reddening light of dawn. Thorny Woods saw him.

"Yuh saved us, Mister Masked Rider," the old man cried. "I savvy yuh caught them skunks in their own trap, 'stead of us. Have yuh seen anything of Louise, my grand-daughter? She's dropped outa sight; we thought they'd brought her thisaway."

The Masked Rider shook his head. But now, he guessed, he knew where Vernon Flynn must have gone. The Chief had snatched the young woman and spirited her off.

"How'd yuh happen to let 'em take her?" he asked, in disguised, gruff voice. The black hat brim shaded the masked face, the cloak was drawn up over his chin. None recognized the mysterious Robin Hood outlaw as the waddy, Wayne Morgan.

Woods, sitting his horse at the distance the Rider seemed to desire, explained.

"A boy come up to our nawth guards, handed in a note an hour back. 'Twas addressed to Louise, from that young dude Bob Harrison. Asked her to come out quiet like and meet him at the main trail. Well,

164

she done it, and I found the note after she'd gone. One of them coyotes yelled at us from the bush that they had Louise, so we sashayed out after 'em."

The Masked Rider's eyes burned through the slits in the domino mask. His lips were grim, a straight line that threatened for Vernon Flynn, devilish chief of this far-flung plot to drive the ranchers from their lawful heritage.

The light was growing brighter. The Masked Rider, with a wave of his arm, swung Midnight and galloped around the edge of the crater, where wounded still writhed in agony. He called, and Blue Hawk swung in ahead of him on the gray. Together they sped up a trail toward the east-and-west road which led from the Ruby Hills to Mescal town.

Where the ranch trail joined the road, the two expert trackers paused, looking for sign. The way was clogged by hundreds of hoofprints, many of them fresh, but they were able to pick out several at the sides where grass still slowly rose into place.

"Go Mescal," grunted the Indian.

Morgan nodded.

"We go now, Senor?"

"Not yet, Blue Hawk. Reckon that sidewinder Flynn won't harm the girl, not for a while. He means to use her against Harrison. And that's why I got to check up again at Lobster Jake's mine. Let's be ridin'. Gotta know why Grole was scairt of rilin' Bob Harrison!"

They heard the voices of approaching cowmen, coming to hunt on the main road in an attempt to track Louise Woods. The Masked Rider swung Midnight's head west, and, the sun throwing their shadows ahead of them, they sped toward the Ruby Hills.

The sun was a brilliant yellow, blinding globe overhead, sending streams of perspiration down the faces of the two men as the Masked Rider and Blue Hawk pushed their lathered horses up the pine-covered, rocky mountainside toward Lobster Jake's gold mine.

Blue Hawk had his instructions. He rode silently at ease, his black eyes alone showing his tense watchfulness, darting from rock to rock, from bush to bush as he scanned the trail ahead for possible ambush.

Working up to the cliff where they had had such a narrow escape from death the night Morgan checked up on the gold deposit, they left their horses and crept forward to look down into the narrow gulch from which the mine opened into the hillside.

There was a man on guard, sitting with his back to the red rock wall, but he was not very alert. He had a half-empty whiskey bottle at his knee, and a ring of cigarette stubs lay about his hobnailed, heavy boots.

"We'll git him, and quietly," whispered the Masked Rider, and Blue Hawk touched the hilt of his long knife.

Dimly they could hear voices of men around the bluff, the miners of Lobster Jake Worrell. Many were with their boss but plenty had remained at camp. The sentry below, his Winchester leaning against the rock near at hand, closed his eyes, nodding for a moment, then jerked awake again to take another pull on his bottle. There were no miners at work in the shaft; wheelbarrows and tools stood unused close to the adit.

The Masked Rider and his Indian comrade took a lariat and began crawling toward a spot which would bring them directly above the sentry at the mine mouth. They had reached a point close to their unsuspecting prey when shots and sudden yells rang out in the encampment. The Masked Rider drew back, a hand on Blue Hawk's lean-muscled brown arm. "Down," he murmured, and they flattened themselves on the rocks overhead as the guard leaped to his feet and grabbed up his rifle.

A man dashed into view, around the red bluff toward the camp. He was running with the speed of a panic-stricken deer, feet flying over the rough path. He turned to look back over his shoulder, and Morgan glimpsed the pallid, sweat-covered face. A rough bandage had slipped off his cheek, showing knife scars scarcely scabbed over. Bullets whirled after the fleeing man, cutting the edge of the bluff and spurting up shale behind him, but he had made the corner and was rapidly heading up the narrow gulch past the mine.

It was David Rose, the Chicago Mining Company expert assayer. He was running for his life, and his breath came in awful gasps, arms flying in the speed of his motion.

Down low as they now were pressed, the Masked Rider and Blue Hawk could not see the rifleman at the mine entrance. It was not till they heard the sudden crack of the Winchester, saw Rose stumble, fall, roll head over heels on the red shale, that they realized how far the miners meant to go. Rose lay quiet as the mob of miners, brandishing clubs and pistols, hustled up on his trail and grouped around him.

Lobster Jake Worrell did not appear. A

burly hombre with a black beard knelt over the assayer, feeling his heart. The man who had been on duty at the mine came into the Masked Rider's vision.

"Yuh damn fool," growled the burly lieutenant, "yuh've kilt him."

"Well, I couldn't help it," the guard replied sullenly, voice thick with liquor. "I jist meant to wing him, that's all."

"He jumped up and run for it while we was eatin'," the burly fellow explained. "Pick him up, boys, and carry him back to the tent. I hope Jake and the Chief won't be mad."

Their ears filled with sounds of heavy boots on the sliding red shale, talking excitedly over the shooting, the gang of miners lifted the dead man and returned to camp around the canyon bend. The sentry shrugged, turned and resumed his guard. He reseated himself on his flat rock, leaning his deadly rifle against the wall.

The Masked Rider, suspicions fully confirmed, edged to position directly over the unsuspecting sentry. Quickly he made a running noose in his lariat and, with a practiced flick of his supple wrist, dropped it over the killer guard's head. Tightening it in a fraction of a second, cutting off the startled cry that rose in the man's throat as he raised his head, the Masked Rider let the rawhide bite deep into the villain's throat. A dull snap sounded as the Rider put his two hundred pounds into the yank, almost falling backward as he hanged the killer of Rose, lifting him clear of the ground so that he dangled against the red cliff, chin touching his breast, tongue sticking out as he died.

"That's one the law won't hafta hang," muttered the Masked Rider.

He fastened the end of the rope to a protruding rock, and nodded to Blue Hawk. The Yaqui, Winchester ready in hands, knelt on the cliff brink as the Rider quickly descended the rope to the mine entrance. On guard, Blue Hawk watched the bluff, hearing the voices of Lobster Jake's unsuspecting men raised in talk over at the camp.

Minutes passed while the Masked Rider remained in the gold mine. The solemn face of Blue Hawk never changed its set, inscrutable look, his black eyes fixed on the bend in the canyon.

Twenty minutes elapsed. Suddenly the Winchester in the Indian's brown, lithe hands rose, covering the point where the red cliff swung around to the flat on which Worrell's encampment stood. Three men in corduroy, caps, and jack-boots came striding toward the mine. They were chatting together, unaware of the Masked Rider's presence, or of the silent Indian figure on the cliff top.

Then one saw the dangling corpse of the sentry.

"Hey — look!" he gasped, stopping in his tracks to point a stubby, dirty finger at the startling sight.

"By Gawd, somebuddy's hung Jepson!" shouted a second. "Hey, boys — c'mon, quick — bring yore guns! There's spies up here."

CHAPTER XV
GOLD FEVER

Rushing forward, the trio dug for their irons, hobnailed boots sliding on the shale as they started for the black hole in the cliff. Blue Hawk's Winchester spat once, and the long bullet caught the leading miner in the left shoulder, spun him around, knocking him head over heels as he shrieked with pain and shock.

The other two paused, bringing their Colt revolvers up and letting go. Bullets whistled around the Yaqui's dark head, bound with its crimson sash, but he was unmoved. The rifle spoke a second time. Blue Hawk never missed with his favorite weapon. A second miner took lead, doubling up with hands clutching at his belly. The third, with a yelp of terror, tossed away his gun and turned tail, running back to meet the oncoming miners from the camp.

The Masked Rider bounded from the mouth of the gold mine, quickly took in the situation, came swarming up the taut lariat to Blue Hawk's side.

"There they are — git 'em!" shrieked a man in the lead of the miner pack.

Guns barked a fusillade, bullets whining in the air, and slapping off the red stone. The Masked Rider and Blue Hawk returned the fire, cutting down two in the van of the miners, forcing the others to stop and hunt cover.

They retreated back across the top of the bluff, found their horses, mounted and started down the mountain, out of the Ruby Hills.

A trickle of blood ran down the Masked Rider's left cheek, where a revolver bullet had burned past him.

"Senor," murmured the Yaqui, unperturbed by the swift, sharp fight, "you find what you wish?"

"Yeah, I found it, Blue Hawk. Just what I figgered."

Far behind them roared the furious baffled crew they had stirred up. Shouts of hatred rang in the hot dry air. Fruitless bullets sang above them, whining ominously as they descended the slopes.

"Now for Mescal," announced the Masked Rider. "That's where we make our last play, win or lose, Blue Hawk. Vernon Flynn's there, and I think Lobster Jake is, too. And Ike Norton, the land commissioner. I figger on takin' care of him. He's another of Flynn's lieutenants."

Blue Hawk nodded, long face expressionless. He looked back once toward the canyon in which lay the gold men had died for. The greedy, rapacious ways of white men were beyond him.

Swift as they rode, the run to Mescal town consumed long hours, and took hard pushing. Halting a mile west of the town, the Robin Hood outlaw changed from his dark Masked Rider costume to that of the wandering waddy he assumed when he wanted to contact people. He traded horses with Blue Hawk, who dropped a short way to the rear of Midnight.

Morgan was guiding the gray horse down the hill which led finally to Main Street, when suddenly he reined in, hand dropping to a heavy Colt butt. Then he recognized the hearty voice hailing him, and old Jim Thorny Woods stepped out of the bush at the south side of the road, waving to him.

"Howdy, Morgan! Yuh shore kin crop up, and drop outa sight at funny times. Where yuh bin?"

"Oh, ridin' the bush. What goes on?"

Woods was worried, face drawn, lines of

pain about his grim, cracked lips, though he held himself with a tight rein like the seasoned thoroughbred he was.

"Some of the boys're with me, and I've sent back to the ranch for ev'ry son who kin ride," he explained. "My granddaughter has been kidnaped and they brought her this-away, 'cordin' to the tracks we picked up. Town's full of gunmen, and the roads are blocked. When we tried to fight our way in, I got a message sayin' Louise wouldn't be hurt if we stayed off, but that if we made trouble she's good as dead."

Wayne Morgan knew who had written that note. Vernon Flynn, the master criminal he was closing in on as perpetrator of the murderous plot against the cowmen. Pat Grole, Lobster Jake, Norton — these, Morgan had deduced were only tools in the hands of the terrible Chief.

"How many men yuh reckon they got in Mescal?" he demanded.

"A hundred, mebbe more. We busted half of Grole's gang south of the Rabbit Leg, thanks to the Masked Rider; but the rest're in Mescal, armed and dog-eyein' ev'rybuddy who sticks his nose out. Lobster Jake Worrell's there, too, got some of his tough miners with him. And there's a bunch of pilgrims come in, by wagon and hoss.

They look like rushers to me, followin' the gold strike. I s'pose the news has leaked out. They'll be floodin' the district and stakin' claims along the streams."

"And is Bob Harrison in town?"

"Reckon he is. Fust I thought he'd helped take Louise, but I figger it was jist a trick to git her — the writin' on the note that drew her out and the one I got a while back bein' the same. Harrison ain't the sort to pull sich a dirty play."

"Yuh're right. Harrison's a decent young feller, Woods. There's somebuddy else behind this trouble of yores."

Morgan had been in the saddle for many hours with hardly a break; he was exhausted, and must rest. Knowing that he could not enter Mescal in the daylight without being instantly spotted by Flynn's gunnies, he dismounted and led his horse after Thorny Woods to the spot where the ranchers squatted in the chaparral. The men lounged around impatiently, eager to help Louise, but not daring to move yet because of the death threat received.

They had jerked beef, dry bread, and liquor, and freely offered it to Morgan. He ate a meal, borrowed a blanket, and lay down under a bush, to fall quickly into dreamless slumber.

It was dusk when he awoke. The cowmen were chatting in low voices, some of them eating. Morgan, stiff but refreshed by the vital sleep, stood up, stretched himself, had another meal, and strolled over to Thorny Woods. The old brush-popper lay on a blanket near the north end of the hidden camp. He had assembled fifty hard-bitten cowmen who would die to help a friend.

"Woods, I'm goin' into Mescal," Wayne Morgan began. "I kin slip through in the dark without givin' any alarm, and I'll see kin I find where they're holdin' Louise. When yore reinforcements come up, keep 'em here till yuh here from me."

The old, seamed eyes, still filled with courage, sought Morgan's grim, strong ones. Thorny Woods nodded.

"I'll wait a while," he promised at last. "Though it's hard sittin' here, knowin' my girl's in danger."

The tall waddy rose up, stalked to the gray horse. Mounting he headed north to the road. The faithful Blue Hawk hovered close at hand. Like a wraith he appeared at Morgan's low hail.

There were gunmen on the trails which led into Mescal, so they took to the bush, gradually working closer to the town. When they could take the horses no farther without discovery, Wayne Morgan whispered to his Yaqui friend:

"Stay here and hold 'em, Blue Hawk, I'm goin' in."

He crept on to the edge of the chaparral northwest of Mescal, lay flat on his belly and looked over the lighted town. The place hummed with excitement. Grim-faced, heavily armed men stalked the plaza and the walks under the awnings. There were numerous strangers, their packhorses heavily laden. Shovel and pick handles stuck out from blanket rolls, many having flat pans used in washing placer gold from stream sands. The saloons were doing a roaring business.

Ike Norton's square, wooden house was lighted. It was of two stories, facing east across the plaza. Morgan's slitted eyes turned toward it. As he watched, he saw a tiny ruby glow in the shadow by the building — a cigarette end burning high as a man pulled on the smoke. At the back corner he glimpsed a burly, dark figure against the lighter paint on the wall.

"Guarded," he mused.

Suspicion started in his clever brain.

Not far away, at a hitch rack in front of the general store, closed for the night, he saw a burro with a miner's pack on its back.

The owner was no doubt in a saloon, enjoying himself.

Grole's gunmen would recognize Morgan if they looked him over, would know him as a supporter of Woods' ranchers. They were watching for some such trouble. He seized his chance when it came, and flitted over to the little donkey.

Stetson pulled well down over his brow, head down, shoulders drooped, he led the burro along the shaded edge of the plaza. Men glanced at the plodding figure, and the placid burro fooled the gunnies. They took the person leading it for an arriving rusher, and made no closer scrutiny.

Bob Harrison impatiently awaited the coming of Lobster Jake Worrell. He sat at a round table in the rear room they had hired for the evening at the Red Queen saloon.

The young engineer had spent the time since his arrival in Mescal in helping John Keith, attorney for the Chicago Mining Company, to prepare the necessary legal papers for transfer of the gold mine to the C. M. C.

Keith, a small, dried-up man who wore pince-nez glasses, was a trained lawyer. He had come west with David Rose and Harrison and stayed in Mescal, checking up records at the county land office.

"According to the deeds filed, C. M. C. would be safe in taking up the entire range," Keith informed him, as they waited for Lobster Jake's arrival that evening.

"No," contradicted Harrison. "That land really belongs to the cowmen. They've developed it and have lived on it for many years. I'm going to help them keep it, Keith."

The lawyer shrugged. "Very well. But somebody else will clean up a fortune if we don't. You're missing a big chance, Bob. And suppose this Worrell and his friends refuse to sell you the mine on the terms we have agreed on offering?"

Harrison shrugged. "I'll protect Woods and the cowmen, Keith, and I mean to protect my company as well. The lawless conditions here are such that we've got to take special precautions. So I'll make the offer to Worrell as we agreed. I've been warned to watch my step, and what I've seen going on makes me doubly wary —"

"Someone's coming now," broke in Keith.

The door into the hall which led to the main saloon, which was noisy with voices and music, stood partially open, but the two Chicago Mining Company representatives sat back out of the range of vision of anyone coming from up front. A lamp burned on the round table where Keith had his papers spread out, pen and ink for signatures.

Then an excited voice called from the hallway, "Worrell — Worrell!"

The heavy tread, approaching the room where Harrison and Keith were, paused, and the voice of Lobster Jake replied.

"What yuh want, LaSalle," he growled.

Bob Harrison's fists clenched. The rival buyer, agent for the Arizona Syndicate, was making himself very disagreeable in trying to beat Harrison out in the rush for the Ruby Hills.

"Shhh," warned Keith, finger to lips, "let's hear what he's got to say, Bob."

They kept quiet, and LaSalle's eager tones reached them clearly enough, though he kept his voice down.

"Worrell, I've just received a reply to my telegram. My syndicate will buy your mining claim. I'm authorized to go as high as half a million dollars, and I can pass you, at once, fifty thousand dollars in cash for yourself if the purchase goes through for my company."

Lobster Jake whistled. "Yuh mean that, LaSalle?"

"I certainly do. I'll see that you get your rake-off."

181

"But how can I squirm outa the Chicago Company's option?" demanded Worrell, his voice greedy.

"Our attorneys will take care of that," said LaSalle persuasively.

With a muttered curse, Bob Harrison leaped up, threw off Keith's restraining hand and stepped out into the corridor.

LaSalle started, then scowled at him, sharp face reddening at sight of his competitor. He stuck a hand into his jacket pocket, and Harrison saw the bulge of the pistol. Up the hall slouched Oley King, the assayer.

"I heard you trying to bribe Worrell, LaSalle," snapped Harrison. He shoved past the squat, fiery-faced mine boss to confront his opponent. "You can't get away with it. I've got first crack at that mine with the option Worrell sold me."

"Damn you," gasped LaSalle, furious so young a man had beaten him. "I'll —"

"Hey, take it easy," cried Worrell, stepping to intervene.

Harrison's right hand flew out, gripped LaSalle's wrist. He jerked the man's hand from his pocket, and the taut fingers of the Arizona Syndicate representative brought along a nickel-plated .32 revolver with a snub muzzle. The engineer wrested away the gun, and it hit the floor with a thud.

Oley King lurched forward, but Lobster Jake Worrell beat him to it, setting his broad body in front of the giant Swede.

"Keep back, King," growled Worrell.

The big fellow hesitated, staring at the tough, squat miner. Lobster Jake was an experienced rough-and-tumble fighter, and armed as well. Bob Harrison slung LaSalle off, the tall man bouncing against the wall, stopping when he came up against his friend King.

"Stay away from me, LaSalle," Harrison said thickly, inwardly struggling to control the instinctive fury roused in him by La-Salle. The man felt cold, reptilian to his touch, and he knew he had never hated anyone as much as he did the Arizona Syndicate representative.

Albert LaSalle swore at him, but made no further attempt to attack. Instead, he swung and walked back into the main room of the Red Queen.

Worrell grinned broadly at Bob. "C'mon, young feller, let's have a drink. Nobuddy kin bribe Jake Worrell, and besides, I'll make more, I figger, sellin' to you fellers than to the Arizona. I got an interest in that mine. My backers jist pulled into town and they'll be here in a few minutes. I'll be glad when this monkey bus'ness is done, so's I kin go on a real spree."

Chapter XVI
Morgan's
Accusation

In the room Harrison introduced Worrell to John Keith, and drinks were brought to them from the bar. Ten minutes later four well dressed men in Eastern getup arrived, and Worrell named them as his backers, friends who had grubstaked him.

"Now, gentlemen," began Harrison seriously, "the first assay reports made by our man, David Rose, are very favorable. Mr. Keith here has checked your titles and says they seem in good order. Ordinarily we could close this deal tonight, but the country's in such a state of lawlessness, with so many disputes about title raging, that we feel we've got to take extra precautions to protect our company. I can offer you a round million dollars for the mine, two hundred and fifty thousand down, and the balance in short-term notes."

Worrell heaved a deep sigh. "How yuh mean to pay this quarter million?"

"By check, on Houston. You know the bank here doesn't carry enough cash to handle such a transaction at short notice. Houston is only two days away and our main Chicago office has designated it as the place to pay off, as our chief banking firm has a branch there."

Lobster Jake looked around at his circle of backers, who nodded their approval, and turned back to the speaker. "Okay, let's have the check, Harrison," he agreed.

"There's one condition, gentlemen. It's called for because of the lawless routine in this section and also because this is a large transaction, even for our company. And I will tell you frankly I've been warned to make sure of what I'm doing in regard to your mine."

Worrell frowned. "What yuh got to say? Go ahead," he urged.

"I don't wish to take any more responsibility or go further," Harrison said decisively, "until my superior in the firm can get here and check the deal. He's starting tomorrow morning and will be here inside a week. This check we'll pass to you now, but I must wire Houston to hold the money in escrow until they hear from us."

"In what?" growled Worrell.

Keith explained. "In escrow means that

the money is there, in the bank, and ready. We can't take it back so long as you follow the conditions in our agreement; on the other hand, you cannot cash the check without a written release from us."

"Huh." Worrell was plainly upset. "I got a good mind to take LaSalle's offer. But wait a jiffy. I got a lawyer friend outside who'll tell me jist what to do." He jumped up and hurried along the hall.

When he returned, within a few minutes, he was smiling. "Okay, Harrison, we'll accept yore offer. Yuh'll be wirin' Houston not to let us have the cash till they hear again from you, but it's there aw right?"

"Yes, you can check that up. I'll telegraph tonight. So can you."

"It's a deal."

Necessary papers were signed, attested. Keith passed the draught on the Houston bank to Lobster Jake and his friends. Notes were prepared for the balance. A final round of drinks was brought to celebrate the transaction. They were halfway through when a shot crackled in the alley outside.

"Town's fulla rushers," remarked Lobster Jake, settling back in his chair. "Reckon some of 'em are drunk and startin' to fight."

"If they buy up any range land," said Harrison, "they'll find they're cheated. Those cowmen have a valid title, in my opinion. I'm going to warn the rushers in the morning."

Worrell shrugged. "That's nothin' to me, Harrison. All we was interested in was the mine itself. Let 'em fight it out. But yore company'll need that land for a reservoir and right-of-way for a railroad spur if yuh wanta develop big."

"I'll take care of all that," promised Harrison, "and see that the rightful owners aren't cheated."

"Yuh've done a smart job, gittin' this mine," Worrell complimented. "It's the richest lode I ever come across."

Harrison stood up. "I'd better be getting to the telegraph office. I don't think your money will be held in escrow more than a week. Do you want to —"

Half a dozen pistols exploded right outside the window, cutting him off. There was cursing and stamping of feet. Then the back door burst in. Harrison, jumping to the hall door, saw the waddy he knew as Wayne Morgan, the man who had helped out Thorny Woods. A bullet thudded into the door frame, and Morgan, with surprising litheness for such a big man, leaped into the hall, slamming the thick oak door shut, bolting it.

"Hello," Harrison exclaimed. "What's wrong?"

As Morgan turned, Harrison saw spreading blood fresh on his left shirt sleeve. The face was grimly set, and he gripped a Colt in his right hand from which a wisp of gray smoke slowly rose. Men were banging lustily on the door, and someone tried to shoot through it, as Morgan glided up the corridor and stepped into the conference room.

Lobster Jake swore hotly at this intrusion, but the broad-shouldered waddy had his Colt up and stood just inside the doorway, from which point he covered the roomful of men.

"What's wrong, Morgan?" demanded Harrison again, frowning.

"I bin huntin' yuh, Harrison," Morgan drawled. "The town's fulla gunmen, and keepin' outa their way's made me late. I just made the back alley here when some of 'em spotted me and started at me. They're coverin' this place."

Harrison looked perplexed. He watched the strong face of the tall hombre. "You were hunting me?"

"Yeah. Have yuh bought that gold mine yet?"

"We've just signed the papers and passed a check — though the money's to be held for a week in Houston."

"Yuh better stop payment and call the whole deal off," said Morgan coolly.

Lobster Jake swore, took a step toward the man at the door.

"Yuh're loco!" he snarled. "Git out before I —"

The Colt barrel centered its single, menacing eye on the squat, crimson-skinned miner.

"Stand quiet and keep yore hands away from yore gun, Worrell," ordered Morgan. "Harrison, yuh've bin cheated, and cheated bad. Lucky no money's passed."

"How so?" demanded Harrison incredulously. He liked Morgan, knew him to be a friend of Thorny Woods. He looked honest and decent and his words carried conviction. Harrison was glad he had taken the precaution of not paying over any cash money save for the initial option.

"That mine is salted," Morgan stated bluntly.

"Impossible!" exclaimed Harrison. "Why, they might fool me by such a trick but they could never put it over on David Rose. He's the smartest assayer in the country."

"He isn't," replied Morgan grimly. "He *was*. He's dead, Harrison, murdered by Worrell's fake miners. Those fellers ain't

190

really miners; they're gunmen Grole and a sidewinder called Vern Flynn brought in here."

"Yuh're a liar!" shouted the furious Lobster Jake.

"Rose — dead? Why he was all right when I left," stammered Harrison. "How could they fool him? He'd have told me of anything fishy up there —"

"He didn't dare. It was while you was out that Rose started to make a keerful inspection of that mine. Worrell beat him up and skeered him. Threatened him with torture and death if he didn't make a glowin' report to yuh. I was up there yesterday. I got into that mine and made a close check. It's salted cleverly; they used several thousand dollars wuth of virgin gold. I've seen the trick before; it's bin done plenty of times. Yuh savvy yoreself that saltin' in the right way will fool an expert for a while."

Harrison was bewildered. His face burned, and he couldn't think straight for a moment. Then he gasped, "Why, yes, you're right, Morgan. I do know of a number of cases in which salted gold lodes were bought."

"Shore, they hammer soft gold into veins, and they also shoot it into rotten quartz with shotguns. That's the way it was done up there. At fust look it fooled yore assayer. It would have fooled me on'y I was leery of Worrell and his crew. They hooked up here, as I said, to a crook named Vernon Flynn, the chief of all this hell. It was all Flynn's idea — Worrell, Grole, and Ike Norton in on it as his helpers."

Lobster Jake was shaking with a fury he couldn't control. The saliva dripped from his twisted mouth, and his eyes fairly shot sparks of hate.

"Yuh lyin' skunk!" he gasped. "He's loco, Harrison, I tell yuh. Go on up, check the mine agin yoreself. LaSalle'll buy it if yuh don't wanta."

Keith spoke icily. "Telegraph Houston at once, Bob, order that no draughts be paid. This certainly requires looking into."

"Go to it," growled Worrell. "Yuh'll find Morgan's crazy. Some trick the cowmen've put him up to, I reckon."

Then the mine operator raised his voice, roaring in anger at Wayne Morgan again:

"Damn yore meddlin' heart and soul! I got a mind to —"

The man Bob Harrison knew as Wayne Morgan ignored Worrell and whirled on the balls of his feet. The hall resounded with heavy steps, filling with the gunmen who had smashed in the back door, and others who pushed in from the saloon up front.

As Morgan swung his Colt off Jake Worrell, the red-faced miner made his play for the pistol at his wide waist. His hairy paw clawed at the walnut butt, the weapon flashed out. With a curse, Bob Harrison lashed out with his right hand, knocked against Lobster Jake's forearm to turn the Colt.

Wayne Morgan felt the slug burn his boot top. He was already swinging back toward Worrell, as the silent quartet of "backers" dug for their shooting irons, hidden under their black coats. Worrell, in a transport of fury, leaped away from Harrison, and his pistol came up to kill the man who had exposed him. He was determined to finish Morgan.

The waddy's heavy Colt flashed a fraction of an instant before Lobster Jake Worrell's. The miner's second shot slammed into the floor and tore up splinters a foot from Harrison. Morgan's slug hit Worrell in the teeth, ripped through into his brain. The squat miner fell against the table, rocking the lamp crazily.

In that awful moment there was no time to think anything out. Bob Harrison was no gunfighter. He was an honest young fellow without such experience, bewildered by the speed with which these men handled their weapons.

A hoarse cry welled in his throat, a warning to Morgan, who faced the four cronies Lobster Jake had brought with him. The wandering waddy was about to be shot down from behind. Morgan nodded and fired again, as Lobster Jake, dead as a doornail, slumped in a heap under the table. The lamp chimney smashed, the round reservoir base falling to the floor as it rolled off, struck by Morgan's shot. The room was plunged in blackness, rent by the angry howls of gunmen.

"Stop it —" gasped Harrison.

He was unheard in the reigning pandemonium. All about him was the shrieking whirl of bullets, triggered by the quartet who had come in with Worrell. Slugs drove into the walls, passed through the doorway into the hall, and a couple of incoming gunnies were hit by the lead of their friends. Yelps of anguish rang out. The doorway cleared as the attackers stepped back, shooting into the room in rage.

"Morgan — where are you?" cried Harrison wildly. "Keith!"

There was no reply. The young engineer threw himself flat on the floor to avoid stray bullets. They weren't after him, but he was blinded by the roaring red flashes as the killers hunted for their victim, Morgan.

Yells came from the spot where the four were banging away. One let his gun fall; another thudded heavily to the boards. The other pair, feeling the whirling lead that came from their flank, suddenly quit and bounded for the door.

In that instant, Wayne Morgan showed against the glow of the window which gave out on the alley.

"C'mon, Harrison," he shouted.

Bob Harrison crawled toward the window, intent on getting out of this inferno. The waddy had smashed the glass with his gun barrel end, was climbing through. Outside shots rang out, as though they sought to hold the elusive Morgan. Then he was gone, and his Colts were talking again, driving dismay to the hearts of the hired murderers.

The moment for Harrison to escape passed. Morgan was down out of sight, his pistols barking as he drove a hole through his enemies.

Men were piling into the room, cursing, armed fellows. Matches were struck as guns were shoved against Harrison and John Keith, who was flat on his face under the table, trembling with excitement at the nearness of death.

"Take the two of 'em across the way. Don't let anybody see you," a thin, cold voice commanded. "Blindfold 'em, boys."

"Okay, Flynn!" was the terse answer.

Harrison turned, trying to see this Flynn, who was the leader of these gunnies. The bodies of armed hombres blocked his vision, but he glimpsed a peaked hat, a Mexican sombrero, and fierce eyes, with a red bandanna drawn up to them. Then he was struck alongside the head by a Colt barrel and jolted to his knees.

Brain dizzy, head ringing from the hard blow that had cut the skin, Harrison staggered as his wrists were twisted behind him, and bound. He tried to yell, to fight them, but they beat him down till he could no longer struggle. A gag was thrust into his mouth, and a blindfold tied across his pain-filled eyes.

Gun muzzle digging cruelly in his back, Harrison was hurried through bunches of gunmen to the rear door and out into the night.

CHAPTER XVII
AT NORTON'S HOME

Morgan, breath rasping through his powerful lungs, could not wait to bring Bob Harrison out of that chamber of horror. Instants meant the difference between life and death, and he had to stay alive, to win for the unfortunate ranchers of Chaparral County by balking the plans of Vernon Flynn.

Heavy Colts roaring, he rolled the bunch of gunnies back from the mouth of the alleyway, seeming impervious to the wild bullets singing through his Stetson, cutting his clothes, nipping at his flesh. More men were heading in from the street. Flynn had his killers teeming in the neighborhood of the Red Queen, evidently waiting for him. Exit cut off at both ends of the narrow alleyway, he took the only chance of escape left. Smashing the glass of a window in a darkened building opposite, he dived through into the house across from the Red Queen.

The mob was howling on his trail, shooting blindly. Their lead bit deep into the ledge of the window, roaring into the walls of the house. Morgan picked himself up, bleeding, ran across the darkened room, stumbling against a chair, toward the opposite window opening. He threw up the sash, climbed out into a shadowed side way, ran for the front sidewalk.

The street was thick with people, hurrying toward the Red Queen, center of the hubbub. He paused behind a big barrel set at the corner to catch rain water for use in case of fire, refilling his Colts, and watching his chance. It was easy then for him to slip into the flowing stream of humanity. He was pushed along with the citizens for a few steps as he shoved across and ducked under the hitchrail. Crossing the street to the plaza, he stood at the edge of the open area for a time, watching the surging multitude.

A tall devil with slitted eyes, wearing a prominent pearl-handled six-shooter that he seemed eager to use, stalked down the plaza toward him. He stared curiously at the battered figure of Wayne Morgan.

"What the hell yuh doin' here —" he began. In the light coming from across the dirt road, he saw the grim face of the man standing there. "Why damn you!" he shouted, grabbing at his pearl-trimmed Colt.

Morgan fired, and the tall man sagged, grabbing at his gun arm, mouthing curses at the man who had winged him. He fell to his knees, but came up running. Zigzagging, he began shouting at the top of his voice for help.

Morgan swung, face bleak, and hustled across to the other side of the plaza to disappear between buildings. The chaparral was not far off, and he hit it, calling for Blue Hawk.

Connecting with the Yaqui, he quickly accepted his friend's help in binding the worst of his wounds. Then, changing to the black costume and mask of the Masked Rider, Morgan gave his comrade orders, and headed back into Mescal.

They were hunting for Morgan, warned by the hombre he had winged. Armed men, many mounted, swarmed through Mescal. Citizens and rushers stayed out of the way, unaware of what it was all about.

The black-clad outlaw moved stealthily through the bush, until he was as close as he could get to Ike Norton's home. Lights shone in the place, and he could see the outline of the patrolling guard at the rear as a Stetson loomed against the back windows.

The sentry, one of Flynn's gunmen, met at the corner with another who walked the side; he came back, and met a third who covered that flank.

The Masked Rider, down low, flitted from bush to bush, made the stable and crept along the shadowed wall until he was within a few yards of the guard. For half the distance along the rear of the house the sentry had his back to the spot where the Rider lurked. Seizing his chance, the Robin Hood outlaw ran lightly forward, feet making no sound in the dirt of the yard.

There was a small entry at the back, and he could see the rear door beyond. He reached the stoop before the guard made the corner and turned. Inside the entry, squeezed back out of sight behind the projection of the wooden frame, he let the gunny pass him, then softly tried the knob.

It opened at his touch fortunately, and he stepped into the kitchen. There was no lamp in the room, but light came from the larger chamber beyond the connecting doorway. The Masked Rider tiptoed over, listened, heard voices from up front.

Close at hand showed a narrow stairway, leading to the upper floor. The Masked Rider went up it, pausing temporarily as a step creaked under his weight. At the top he peeked along a hall off which several rooms opened. To the right he saw a tough looking man, with a Colt lying by his knee, sitting on the floor with his back to the wall. He was smoking and looking toward the front of the house.

The Rider's Colt, gripped in his strong hand, hammer back under thumb joint, covered the hombre as he softly climbed the last steps. He was within four feet of the room guard when the fellow turned his head and saw the terrifying figure of the black-clad Rider upon him.

"The Masked Rider!" he gasped.

"Quiet! If yuh yell or move yuh're a dead man," snarled Morgan.

The gunman froze, limbs stiff with fear. His eyes rolled in his head at sight of this fighting Robin Hood who stood so mysteriously between the hordes of Vernon Flynn's killers and the cowmen of Chaparral County.

The room door was locked but the key was outside, in the hole. Holding the gunman pinned with his pistol, the Masked Rider felt for the key with his free hand, turned it, started backing into the dark chamber.

"Aw right — stand up slow and keep yore hands high," he growled. "Come in here."

The gunny obeyed, knowing he would die if he balked this determined man. Closing the door, the captor struck a match. The glow showed the room, with its furniture. On the bed, gagged and trussed, lay Bob Harrison. His eyes rolled toward the dark figures by the door, and the Masked Rider saw that the young engineer still lived.

A high-pitched voice called from below.

"Devlin, are they both okay?"

The guard glanced helplessly at the grim Rider whose glowing eyes seemed to have eaten the slits in his black domino mask.

"Answer him," hissed the black-clad man, his Colt stressing the order. "Say they are all right."

The gunny's voice broke with fear as he called back, "Okay, Norton."

The captor backed toward the wide bed where Bob Harrison lay, helpless.

"C'mon," he ordered, and the prisoner he had taken followed him, step by step, arms high. The Masked Rider could see him against the lighted oblong of the hall door.

"Take this knife and cut his ropes," he directed. "If yuh so much as look funny I'll drill yuh."

The hombre obeyed, hands shaking with fright. Harrison was quickly freed. He sat up on the edge of the bed, rubbing his cut wrists, and the guard returned the knife at Morgan's command.

"Thanks," Harrison muttered. "They — they beat me up."

"Tie this snake," the Masked Rider snapped, "and let's go. Grab his gun on yore way out."

Harrison swiftly trussed the guard, and the Masked Rider shoved the man to the floor, and glided over to the doorway. He looked up the hall, and saw Ike Norton appear at the head of the front stairs. Something in the guard's voice when he had answered must have made the small county commissioner uneasy, and he was coming up to see for himself that all went well.

He came quickly along the hall toward the room.

"Devlin!" he called querulously. "What are you doing?"

When he was within a few feet, the Masked Rider, gun up, stepped out and confronted him.

"Makin' buzzard meat, Norton," he answered softly.

The tiny Norton recoiled with terror, unable to utter the scream of fear that welled in his throat. With a tigerish bound, the Rider was on him, left hand shooting out to grasp the scrawny throat. Norton fell down, groveling at the masked man's feet. He began begging for mercy in a high-pitched whine:

"Don't kill me, Mister, please, please —"

The gun pointed inexorably down at Norton's brain and the small hombre raised an arm across his eyes as though hoping to shield his head from the tearing bullet.

"Keep yore voice low," snarled the Rider, in a deep and gruff tone that was different from the voice of the waddy Wayne Morgan, a timbre that fitted the desperate guise which he wore.

Bob Harrison still half-dazed from the beating he had taken, steadied himself against the frame of the door, stared at the strange scene as the county commissioner begged mercy. Plainly the thing Ike Norton feared most had come upon him: the Masked Rider, whom he had seen before in action, had him. At each slight movement the outlaw made, Norton cringed in anticipation of death.

"You can't blame it on me, sir," gasped Norton, the floodgate of speech bursting in his nervousness, "Vernon Flynn made me go through with it. He's — he's a hard man, a killer and a criminal — excuse me, I forgot —" His frightened eyes sought the grim eyes through the slits of the domino mask as he recalled that the Masked Rider, too, was an outlaw.

"I mean, the police want him," he hurried on. "He was hidin' down here in the Ruby Hills and got a hold on me, you see. Grole fell in with him right away, and it was all Flynn's idea, formin' the new county and then plantin' that gold in the cave. Lobster Jake knew just how to do it.

"I never wanted to kill anyone, I swear it! But Flynn made me go on and on — to this —" He shuddered. "Woods' girl is all right; she's in the front bedroom. My wife's taking good care of her, watching her. Then he had the young man brought over —"

"Louise — they've got her here?" cried Harrison, suddenly realizing what Norton meant. "Why, damn you, Norton!"

He sprang toward Norton, his hands reaching for the commissioner's scrawny neck. But a gesture of the Masked Rider stopped him.

The voices in the hall had disturbed Mrs. Norton. Her bedroom door, at the front of the second story, clicked open and she looked out upon the scene. She saw the masked man, the guns, and her husband at the mercy of the tall, mighty bandit. Her hand flew to her lips, and she uttered a shrill scream.

There was an answering shout from below. The Masked Rider knew the guards would answer the woman's cry. He swiftly picked up Ike Norton, slung him across his left shoulder, motioned Harrison to follow, growling in a deep voice:

"Yore girl'll be safer here. C'mon, hustle."

Harrison hesitated but an instant. Then he followed the Rider down the back steps. The Robin Hood outlaw, somehow, inspired the respect and obedience of those with whom he came in close contact.

Norton was as nothing to the trained, powerful muscles of the Masked Rider. Burdened though he was, he flung open the kitchen door, stepped into the entry as the shouts of the men Flynn had left on guard sounded about the square house. Up front they were stamping in, guns ready for trouble as Mrs. Norton screamed to them. The sentry on duty at the rear of the place ran toward the entry where the Masked Rider stood, Norton across one shoulder, heavy black Colt gripped in his right hand.

The gunny was at the bottom of the stoop before he spied the Masked Rider. With a yip of alarm, he tried to throw his pistol up. The gun roared, bullet plugging into the boards between the spread boots of the Masked Rider. Then the outlaw's revolver replied, and the gunman doubled up with a leaden bellyache.

The Masked Rider leaped the quivering body, Harrison jumping after him. Dark figures of gunmen dashed around from both sides, and the Rider slowed, swinging to blast splinters off the corner of the house, while Harrison fired at the other turn. This held pursuit back until the fugitives could make the dark bulk of the stable.

"There they go — it's the Masked Rider!" came frenzied yells.

Harrison ran with the tall outlaw, who held on to the panic-frozen Ike Norton. Ahead loomed the black wall of chaparral, and a low call told the Masked Rider his faithful partner Blue Hawk was at hand. A Winchester glinted blue-black in the sky glow and knifed out a lance of orange flame. The long bullet tore into the massing ranks of gunmen who dared follow.

Then Harrison and Morgan hit the bush, fading back as Blue Hawk's terrible rifle stopped the pursuers for a minute with its accurate, smashing fire.

Not far back stood a saddled horse, brought there by the Yaqui according to Morgan's order.

"Mount and ride," commanded the Masked Rider to Harrison. "Yuh'll find

Woods and his men camped up the hill west of town. Tell 'em the Masked Rider says the time has come to fight. And soon as yuh kin, telegraph Houston to stop payment on that check yuh gave Worrell. Vernon Flynn's got it now."

The incisive, gruff instructions the Rider gave were not questioned. Grateful for the rescue, Bob Harrison nodded, jumped to the saddle of the powerful mount, and rode west along a narrow, winding trail in the bush.

Blue Hawk's Winchester was steadily talking, speaking a language understood by the murderers who sought to catch the black-clad hombre. Three of them lay on the earth and the others, appalled at the deadly accuracy of a marksman who never missed, had taken cover.

Chapter XVIII
Cowmen Fight

Energetically the Masked Rider cut around to the north, to the spot where Midnight and the gray horse stood. He slung Norton a flabby, limp bundle who was past the point of any resistance, across the front of the saddle and began to ride out of the area where bullets blindly sought them, clipping leaves and thudding into dirt, singing through the air. Blue Hawk, below, with a rock for a shield, resumed his firing to draw the attention of gunmen who would bob up now and then to shoot.

The whole town was in an uproar. Some of Vernon Flynn's devils were running toward Norton's home. Others were circling about like beheaded chickens, hunting the cause of the sudden uproar, urged on by long-shanked, cruel-faced lieutenants. Citizens and rushers wisely stayed indoors, or kept out of the way, unaware of the cause of this underground but fierce strife that raged.

At last the Masked Rider with his captive was north of Mescal, well in the chaparral, and hunting a way around toward the massive city hall, that adobe fortress in which reposed the town lockup and the various offices of the new county. Shafts of silver moonlight, piercing the interstices of jungle growth, touched the strong, grim jaw and lit the glowing eyes through the slits of the domino mask.

Ike Norton, slung face down, legs hanging on one side of the powerful black stallion, arms and head down the other shoulder, joggled roughly by the motion, was scratched by long thorns as they pushed through the bush. All thought of resistance, of cunning, had fled from Ike Norton. All he hoped for was his life.

The Masked Rider, riding silently, urged the black stallion over east of Mescal, and then found a path back, winding in and out, until he was near to the back door of the fortress. It was here that he had saved the cowmen chiefs from the killers who sought to drygulch them as they left the jail.

He dismounted, gave the black animal a pat. Midnight would wait where he was left, or would come at his call. Seizing his prisoner, the Masked Rider flung Ike Norton over his shoulder again, turned and cocked an ear, listening for Blue Hawk.

After a few minutes the wraithlike Indian came riding on his trail, the re-loaded rifle across his saddle horn. Flynn's gunnies had run across the plaza to Norton's place and were howling and shooting at shadows in the bush there. Blue Hawk needed no further instructions. He slipped from the saddle and silently flitted toward the back door of the city hall.

Blue Hawk pried the portal open, disappeared inside. After a quick survey, he showed in the rectangle once more, a white arm signaling the Masked Rider that all was clear. Carrying Norton, the black-clad outlaw trotted across to join the Yaqui. Together they went up the dark hall, turned into the land office.

The black-clad hombre motioned to Blue Hawk, who shut and bolted the door into the corridor. The Masked Rider let Ike Norton slide to the floor, and the commissioner lay there in the dim room, eyes wide and staring as he watched the lithe movements of the utterly soundless Yaqui. He saw the long knife in the sash, the dark, fierce face hardly visible.

The Masked Rider took a candle stub

from his pocket, shaded the match with his hand as he lighted the blackened wick stub. Blue Hawk knelt beside the crooked commissioner. Knife drawn, he extended his long brown arm until the razor sharp blade touched Ike Norton's quivering throat.

From the darkness, his eyes blinded by the yellow glow of the candle which was close to his face, Ike Norton heard the gruff command of his terrible Nemesis.

"Take yore pen and git busy, Norton."

"What — what d' you want me to do?" gasped the little hombre.

"Change the records yuh cheated on. Gimme them dummy deeds to burn, and file the rightful claims of the ranchers."

"All right — I'll do anything you say. Only — only call *him* off!"

He pointed a trembling finger at the Yaqui. To Norton, Blue Hawk was chiefly that fang-like knife. To his raw, hypersensitive nerves, torture and death were on him, and he felt his bones turning to gelatine. A haze of redness dimmed his vision.

By the light of the single candle, shaded by the desk and the black-dressed body of the Masked Rider, Ike Norton set to work on the land records. His hand trembled so he could hardly write, but he knew that implicit obedience was his one chance of

212

life, and he worked with a desperate speed.

Neither Morgan nor Blue Hawk spoke while Ike Norton undid the crooked recording work to which Flynn had egged him on.

"There," said Norton at last, blinking as he looked at the shadowy form of the Masked Rider. "That's about all. Will you let me go now?"

"Purty soon."

Dimly, from the plaza, came the sounds of renewed gunfire, the fierce cries of fighting men.

"Thorny Woods is in," muttered the Masked Rider. "C'mon, Blue Hawk. Fetch that little rat."

Unbolting the door into the hall, the Robin Hood outlaw peered up and down to find the way clear. He could hear the battle outside warming up with heavy shooting and yells of furious hombres.

Blue Hawk moved silently forward as the Masked Rider signaled him.

"Git a rope and all yore rifle ammunition," ordered the black-clad man in a low voice.

Norton caught at the word "rope." He gasped, "You — you ain't goin' to hang me — after I did everything you told me to. You —"

"Take it easy. Yuh're safe — long as yuh

behave," the Masked Rider told him contemptuously.

He picked Norton up, shouldered him, toted him to the stairs. "Go ahead, git on upstairs."

Blue Hawk came back, pockets sagging with Winchester shells, lariat drooped over one arm. He trailed the Masked Rider and Norton to the second floor. Ike Norton went up the ladder like a monkey at the Rider's command, emerging on the flat roof.

Powder smoke and dust lay thick against the light glow of Mescal town. Hoarse cries, explosions of rifles, shotguns and pistols, rang out, accompanied by the thud of beating mustang hoofs.

Swiftly Wayne Morgan trussed Ike Norton and left him lying at the side of the roof, under the protection of the parapet. With the Yaqui at his heels, he crossed to the front and looked down on the plaza.

To the west he could see the array of fighting ranchers, with their waddies and friends. All were mounted, save for those who had taken crippling lead and fallen from their saddles. Old Thorny Woods was leading them, bellowing his orders. Spread out, they were fighting Indian fashion and speeding up and down where there wasn't any cover, and slowly but inexorably advancing into town.

Vernon Flynn's array of gunfighters had backed across the plaza, lining up on the east side of the square, their rear to the fortresslike city hall. Bunches of bandits squatted behind posts, crouched at the sides of the buildings on the street. Bullets thudded thick into the wood, into the dirt, into exposed shoulders as Flynn's killers sought to pick off the fast-riding cowboys.

Heavy volleys threatened the ranchers out in the open. They were outnumbered by the gunmen, with whom a number of Lobster Jake Worrell's supposed miners had joined, hombres who had ridden from the Ruby Hills as an escort to their deceased leader.

Up on the parapet, behind the murderous array, Blue Hawk and the Masked Rider set themselves in the shadows. The Yaqui's white teeth gleamed, gritted in pleasure as he opened up with his Winchester, stuck through a firing-slit. Every time the rifle spoke, a murderer arched his back, or rolled over with a grunt, out of action.

The Rider's two heavy Colts grew hot in his trained hands as they roared with red flashes of death into the rear and flanks of the killer horde. Hard-faced lieutenants, egging on their men, looked back over their shoulders to see who was shooting with such disastrous accuracy from their rear. The black Stetson, the masked face of Wayne Morgan, showed only for an instant as he bobbed up to empty his Colts down at them.

Quivering flesh shuddered, relaxed as the heavy lead slugs struck home. Both Blue Hawk and his beloved Senor were picking off gunmen lieutenants. Stung by their terrible fire, the killers turned, sought to take out the two on the parapet.

"Go on and bring 'em down!" roared a tall, red-eyed devil. He crashed forward on his face an instant later as the Masked Rider's Colt boomed a reply to his order.

A bunch of men ran through into the city hall. The black-clad outlaw darted back to wait at the trap-door exit while Blue Hawk continued firing. The trap was pushed up from beneath, and the Masked Rider fired. The foremost man yipped, fell down on his mates, and the heavy cover slammed shut again.

Blue Hawk went on calmly picking them off below with his favorite weapon, the deadly Winchester. The Masked Rider flitted back, touched his faithful Indian friend on the shoulder, indicated the trap-door. Blue Hawk nodded, swinging to watch the opening while the other surveyed the progress of the fight. The trap was gingerly raised a second time. The rifle spat, and once more the trap-door dropped. They dared not push it up any more; death awaited the man who attempted it.

Both Colts going, ears singing with the paean of death, the Masked Rider stung the lines of gunmen. The cowboy whooping increased in volume as a crowd of killers to the south of the city hall suddenly jumped up and scattered back through the side alleys in retreat.

"Charge — go git 'em, boys!" roared old Thorny Woods, waving his Frontier Model .45 like a general's sword.

Spurs driven in, the ranchers galloped straight into the faces of the murderous array of fighting bandits used by Vernon Flynn.

The Masked Rider, still picking them off, sought with his keen eyes for a sight of the "Mexican," whom he knew was the ranchers' enemy in disguise.

"Where is that sidewinder Flynn, I wonder?" he muttered aloud as he failed to discover Flynn at all in the fray.

Blue Hawk rejoined him at the front parapet, turning now and then to make sure the men who had sought to get at them from below had really given up their attempt.

The uproar speeded up, increasing in pitch and volume. The battle was at its greatest height in the following moments. Concentrating on the center, the Rider and the Yaqui drove home their lead as the cowmen spurred their mustangs in.

Men died down there, fighting for their homes. They took lead, and fought on when they could. The gunmen wavered, shaken by the fierce fire from the parapet that showed no mercy, no sign of slackening. Then the line of horsemen hit them with an audible clash, and hand-to-hand fighting ensued, slashing with pistol barrels, knives, spurred boots.

The center of the line of gunmen wavered. A man turned, nerve smashed, right arm limp from a Rider .45 bullet. He ran screaming through the alleyway out of sight. Two more followed, making a wide gap. Then the whole line melted away like snow before a hot flame.

The right flank wavered in confusion as the center broke. Then, in the face of those charging horsemen and the deadly fire of the two men on the courthouse roof, the rest of the bunch let go and took it on the run, hunting mounts on which to escape the revenge of the hot-blooded Texans.

A company of cowmen under Thorny Woods leaped off their horses and ducked under the hitchrails, guns gripped in hand, to mop up. They began chasing small gangs of gunmen, running them down in dark corners, to surrender or die. Colt barrels slashed at panic-stricken bandits, who dropped their weapons and cried for mercy.

The heavy volume of shooting faded to scattered bursts, then to single explosions. The acrid powder smoke, mingled with alkali dust, began to clear away, settling back or carried off on the gentle night wind. An awful silence fell upon Mescal, broken only by the gruff voices of Woods' triumphant ranchers and cowboys.

Prisoners were being hunted out of corners and hiding-places, those who had not managed to find horses and ride for the Border. They were herded into the center of the plaza where cowboys guarded them.

Thorny Woods limped out, stood below the fort that was the city hall, and stared up at the dim figures of the two on the parapet. He and his people had seen the black-clad hombre up there, knew the Masked Rider had done much toward winning their battle for them.

He swept his bullet-riddled Stetson from

his white-haired head, waved it in a salute to the Masked Rider.

"Many thanks, Mr. Masked Rider," he cried. "Three cheers for him, boys!"

A hearty roar went up as everybody cheered the mysterious outlaw. The Masked Rider raised an arm high in reply, then melted back into the darkness. He found the sweat-saturated Ike Norton trembling where he had been left.

Squatting beside the little man, he growled, "It's all over but the shoutin', Norton. But the big fish seems to have got away. Where yuh reckon Vernon Flynn has gone?"

Norton, teeth chattering, replied.

"He's ridden on to Houston to cash Harrison's big check."

"Huh. It'll take him two days to get to the city and get his paws on that money! Harrison can wire and ketch him," mused the Rider. "How could he ever hope to get that check cashed?"

He untied Ike Norton, shoved him toward the front parapet, dragging the 40-foot rawhide lariat after them.

Looping the noose under the county commissioner's arms, he lifted Norton up on the edge.

"What — what are you goin' to do? Don't hang me," begged Norton.

"You won't be hurt. Just git down there and tell them people the hull story, savvy?"

Citizens and strangers were gingerly coming out, now the battle was over. Rushers, who sought to buy claims in Chaparral, stood around in curious knots, watching the cowmen with their gunmen captives.

The Masked Rider lowered Ike Norton to earth. The little hombre's dangling feet at last touched the city hall stoop which was raised several steps from the ground.

A growl of anger rose from Woods' men as they saw Ike Norton, the traitor. But a warning gesture and shout from the Masked Rider kept them back, quieted them. Thorny Woods snapped an order to heed the outlaw.

Chapter XIX
End of the Trail

Jerking nervously, Norton began to talk. He told of the salted mine, the plot to gain a great fortune through sale of the Ruby Hills and the fake gold lode to the Chicago Mining Company. He revealed how David Rose had been intimidated by Lobster Jake. He spoke of Vernon Flynn, master plotter behind the whole murderous game.

The cowmen listened, amazed at the terrible deviltry that had so nearly ruined them all and driven them from their homeland. Rushers patted themselves on the back, happy to have their money safe in their belts instead of pocketed by thieves for the sale of worthless placer claims.

"Vernon Flynn planned it all," whined on Ike Norton, narrow face pale as flour. "He got all of us in — Pat Grole, Lobster Jake, and me. He told Grole how to enlist the bandits. He stole several thousand dollars in new gold from the Mexican mines at the

Monterrey smelter to furnish metal for that saltin' Worrell did.

"It was planned well and would've worked out if this Masked Rider hadn't come along and butted in. Grole and Worrell're dead, and I'm with you boys from now on if you'll let me. I changed back all records to the rightful owners. Woods, your granddaughter's safe and sound at my house, across the road. My wife's taken good care of her."

Thorny Woods picked out a bunch of young fighting men to ride for the Ruby Hills to clean up the remaining toughs left there by Lobster Jake Worrell.

"Set a guard on that stolen gold, boys," he growled. "I reckon the reward oughta belong to us, to help pay for the damage Vernon Flynn's devils done us."

Harrison nodded and spoke up.

"My company will be very grateful, Woods. They'll certainly want to give you a boost. I still don't quite understand it all. Charles LaSalle of the Arizona Syndicate and his assayer, King, seemed fooled as much as we were!"

"How 'bout this LaSalle?" Thorny Woods asked Norton. "Where is he?"

"I forgot that," Ike Norton said. "You see, to egg Harrison on, make him believe he had to act fast, Vern Flynn pretended to be this Charles LaSalle. There's no such person, really. King, the Swede, is one of his men. Flynn, as LaSalle, kept bobbin' up near Harrison, as though he was a rival buyer. He fooled Harrison, no doubt of that."

Bob Harrison nodded, astounded. "He did. I believed him. I suppose that 'holdup' he accused me of was part of his game, to give me the chance to 'beat' him to the mine. And all his talk of winning over me, in buying that salted lode, threw dust in my eyes so I never suspected he wasn't a rival buyer. The Arizona Syndicate is a genuine company."

"Where's Vernon Flynn now?" Woods asked Norton.

"He's on his way to Houston to cash the check Keith and Harrison passed over," replied Ike.

"Huh. And I bet onct he got his paws on that money, none of yuh'd ever've got a split," Woods growled. "Yuh was a fool, Norton, to throw in with sich a criminal as Flynn."

A clever leader of men, Woods swung to young Harrison.

"Hustle to the telegraph office, son," he said, "and make shore yore firm stops payment on that check, else Flynn will git away with a fortune, and yuh'll be in trouble with yore company. We'll hafta arrest that sidewinder Flynn, if it's the last thing we do, gents. He can't be left roamin' the range, or nobuddy'll be safe."

Harrison nodded, started south across the plaza. His idea of holding the quarter million in escrow had been a good one; but his capture before he could wire Houston had left a negotiable check in the hands of Vernon Flynn.

"I'll stop him," Harrison muttered. "He can't be so clever if he thinks we won't wire ahead of him."

Late though it was, an operator was in the small shack which housed the telegraph line. Bob Harrison, knocking hard on the flimsy door, heard the man stirring about inside.

"Be with yuh in a jiffy," the operator called.

In the shadow at the side, near a partly open window, stood the black-cloaked figure of the Masked Rider. Off in the bush lurked Blue Hawk, holding Midnight and the gray. The Rider could see Harrison's figure there on the stoop of the telegraph office eager to get over to speak to the dainty young woman who emerged with her grandfather from Norton's house.

The door of the telegraph shack was opened by a man with a green shade over his eyes.

"I want to send a rush wire to the First National Bank in Houston," Harrison said swiftly.

"Okay. Come right in. I'll light up."

Close to the window the Masked Rider watched the match flicker, then saw the bent figure of the operator as the man touched the light to a lamp wick and the room showed clear. There was the telegraph instrument on its table, sender and receiver and the necessary apparatus.

"Reckon this'll stop him," muttered the Rider.

He was about to turn away. Harrison had hastily written his message, the operator was bent over his sending key.

"Dot — dot — dot — dot — dash — dash — dot —"

The Masked Rider, a line deepening between his gleaming, hidden eyes, turned back. For moments he listened. He knew the telegraph code.

"Right," the operator said to Bob Harrison. "It's all in. That'll be two dollars."

Harrison paid and hurried out, to join his sweetheart and Thorny Woods.

The dark-clad outlaw slid around the

226

front of the shack and stepped through the door. The operator looked up upon hearing the creak of a worn board. He swore and snatched at a Colt revolver he had hidden under the counter.

The Masked Rider's pistol barked, and the hombre yipped, his own gun clattering to the floor. The black-clad outlaw was upon him.

"That message yuh just sent was a fake," snarled the Masked Rider. "Flynn put yuh here to stop any alarms!"

Fear streaked across the narrow eyes of the man. The Masked Rider pushed through the gate. He saw a boot toe sticking from under the cot.

"Drag him out," he ordered.

The disguised gunman obeyed. The rightful operator, gagged and tightly trussed, was freed. He began swearing as the bandanna came from his mouth.

"Hustle," ordered the Masked Rider. "Send that message there! It'll stop the men who grabbed yuh."

The operator staggered willingly to his keys. He pulled the switch, began to click. This time it was right to the outlaw's trained ear. But the operator had sent only a word when he looked up at the masked man in dismay.

"The line's dead, Mister!"

Vernon Flynn, master criminal who had engineered the entire bloody plot against the ranchers of Chaparral County, had a long start. But the black-clad Masked Rider on the powerful stallion Midnight rode as he had never ridden before, Blue Hawk galloping at his heels.

Flynn had cut the single copper wire to the outer world. Had it not been for Morgan his ruse of placing a man at the Mescal key would have been successful, giving him time to reach Houston.

"Ev'ry minute is precious, Midnight," muttered the Rider, urging the great black animal on the trail.

The fresh sign he could pick out as he rode, expert eyes on the sandy road through the chaparral leading south toward the railroad. On and on sped the Masked Rider, the Yaqui a hundred yards behind on the gray, pushing through the dust kicked up by Midnight's tearing hoofs.

Vernon Flynn rode ahead, the man who must answer for the awful crimes that had taken place in Chaparral County.

Topping a rise, the Robin Hood outlaw could look down across a rolling valley that cut east and west and through which the railroad builders had laid their tracks.

The smoke of a train coming from the west toward the little station plumed in the sky. And in the air about the Masked Rider hung freshly risen dust.

"He ain't far ahead now," he told the black stallion. "Hit the trail, Midnight!"

The lathered, handsome creature put all he had into a final burst of speed, in the effort to reach the settlement ahead of the approaching train.

There were a few loungers on the wooden platform as the Masked Rider whirled south through the main way of the sleepy little town. Men stared in amazement at the masked, black-clad figure that dashed toward the train, which was slowly pulling out from the shed.

By the platform stood a horse covered with bloody foam, run and gored to the end of its endurance by the brutal Flynn. A pistol spat from a car window. The Rider heard the whir of the close bullet that nipped at his black hat brim.

He crossed the tracks, and Midnight galloped swiftly along the cinders. The Masked Rider reached out to grasp the railing of the rear platform and swung over to the steel step.

"Stay with me, Midnight," he shouted, and the black stallion sped on, riderless, after the moving train.

People gaped at the outlaw, freezing in their seats as they thought a holdup was in progress, but the black-clad hombre ran on through the car, gun in hand, and crossed to the next one.

He leaped through the back entry. A bullet shattered the door glass at his back. Up at the front of the car he saw his man. The tall, slender Vernon Flynn, alias Charles La-Salle, darted a venomous look of hatred from his slate-colored, slitted eyes as he took aim again at the masked outlaw.

The sharp face was transfigured by his fury, fury at the man who had balked him. His dark-brown hair, matted to his dusty brow by sweat, was bare, the peaked hat he had worn now discarded.

"Bandit! Kill him! It's a holdup — the Masked Rider," shrieked Flynn.

He ducked down on one knee for more careful aim. The Masked Rider's slug whipped within an inch of his dropping head. Then the outlaw felt the bite of Flynn's second slug as it tore the flesh of his left thigh. He gritted his white teeth, allowing for the swaying, jolting motion of the train, and leveled down on Flynn. The heavy black Colt spat once, twice.

Flynn fell forward on his hands and knees,

his gun clattering in the car aisle. The Masked Rider's first shot had hit his gun arm; the second had drilled a neat hole between the slatey, furious eyes. Flynn collapsed on his face, lay still. The reports of the big Colts echoed up and down in the confined space of the railroad car.

The masked outlaw, blood dripping from his wounded thigh, ran limping along the car. People drew back, watching him, none offering resistance.

"Holdup!" a man gasped.

But the Masked Rider did not pause until he reached the dead Flynn. He stooped, masked face to the seats. Quickly he found Harrison's check and notes. He tore the papers into pieces, let them snow down over the corpse of Vernon Flynn.

The red emergency cord was overhead. He yanked it with his left hand, and stepped out onto the forward platform. The train had gathered speed, and the giant black stallion was falling behind, but was still coming, picking his way along the right-of-way as best he could, obediently following his master.

The brakes jammed on. The train slowed with jolting jerks, and Wayne Morgan leaped off, rolled over and over into the bush at the side of the track. An excited passenger in another car fired several futile shots from a window at the moving figure of the black-clad Rider.

So the world ran on, thinking the Masked Rider a bandit, unaware of the brave deeds he did in helping the unfortunate.

At his call Midnight swung into the bush, came to his side, and he mounted. He raised his arm high, galloping off out of sight of the train.

From a hilltop north of Mescal town, a black-clad figure sat a great inky stallion. At his side was an Indian in white, with straight hair bound by a bright-colored sash, mounted on a splendid gray animal.

The Yaqui somberly watched his friend, the man he had chosen to follow on the Owl-hoot Trail, the man he knew as Wayne Morgan and whom many people of the great West looked on as a notorious bandit. Only these who had been helped here and there knew the real goodness of the heart of the Masked Rider.

There was a celebration in Mescal town. The victorious ranchers whom Thorny Woods headed were painting the settlement red. It was the wedding day of Louise Woods and young Bob Harrison. The stalwart young engineer was taking his bride East for a visit, after which he had promised to return to the range she loved so well.

Happiness was in the sunlit air; cheering cowboys whooped it up in delight as the handsome Harrison kissed his lovely bride.

Blue Hawk shifted uneasily in his leather; he knew how the man he loved was feeling.

"Such is not for you, Senor," the Yaqui muttered softly.

"No, yuh're right, Blue Hawk. It's not for such as me." There was a sad bitterness in the black-clad man's voice.

Never for him could there be the soft arms of a woman such as Louise Woods, or the peace and quiet of a real home. He was doomed to wander the range forever, until the end.

"Reckon we better report in Oklahoma," he said.

The Masked Rider swung the black stallion, shutting off the view of Harrison's happiness. He did not look back again. Strong jaw set, he rode for new pastures, seeking victims of oppression whom he might help, and leaving behind him the deep gratitude of men he had saved.

We hope you have enjoyed this Large Print book. Other Thorndike, Wheeler, Kennebec, and Chivers Press Large Print books are available at your library or directly from the publishers.

For information about current and upcoming titles, please call or write, without obligation, to:

Publisher
Thorndike Press
295 Kennedy Memorial Drive
Waterville, ME 04901
Tel. (800) 223-1244

or visit our Web site at:

http://gale.cengage.com/thorndike

OR

Chivers Large Print
published by BBC Audiobooks Ltd
St James House, The Square
Lower Bristol Road
Bath BA2 3SB
England
Tel. +44(0) 800 136919
email: bbcaudiobooks@bbc.co.uk
www.bbcaudiobooks.co.uk

All our Large Print titles are designed for easy reading, and all our books are made to last.